HONOR ROLL

KELLY COLLINS

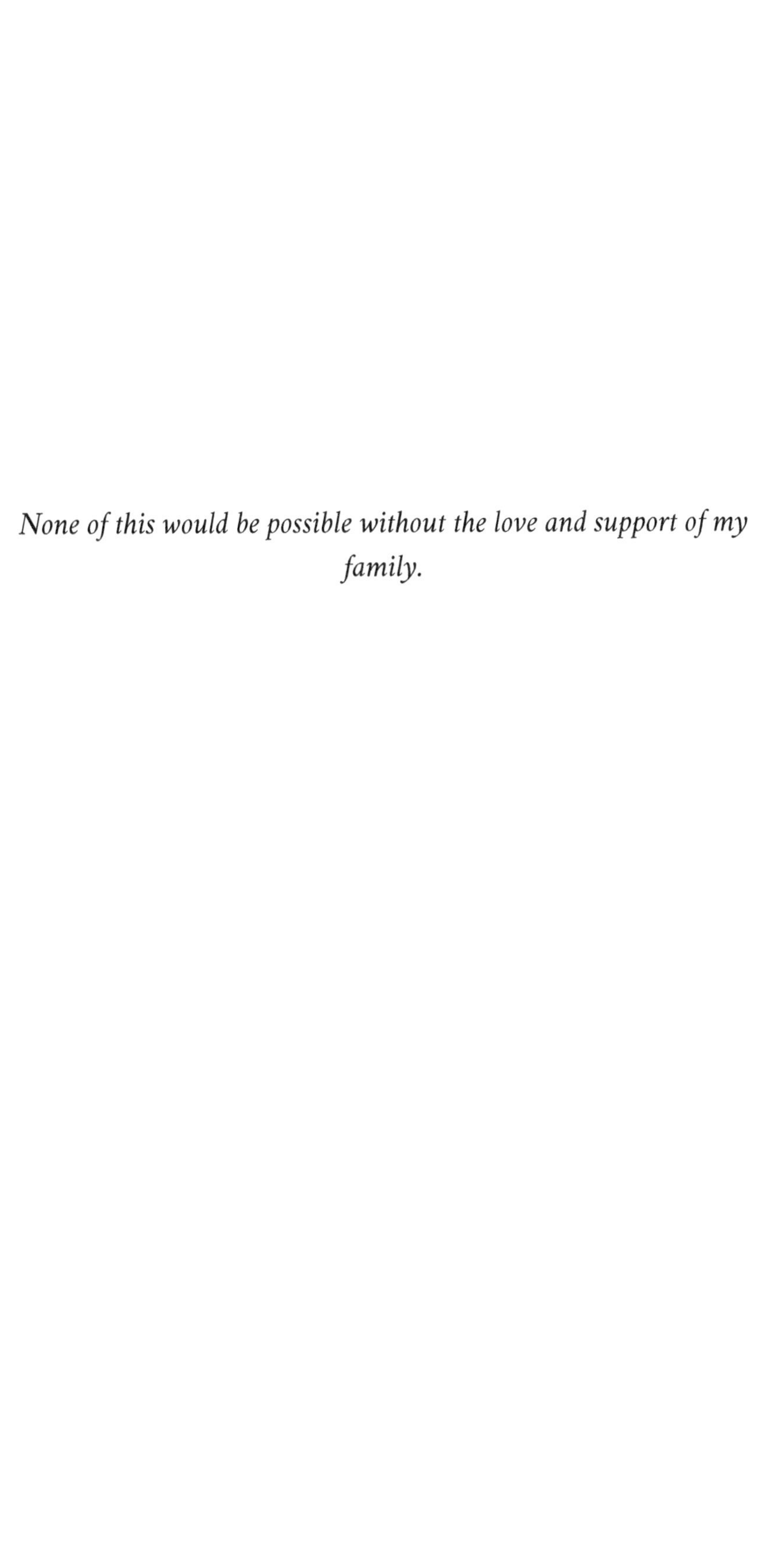

None of this would be possible without the love and support of my family.

Chapter 1

When I stepped off the bus on 6th Avenue, I felt tired. I'd been selling myself by the inch all week, and my twenty-six-year-old body couldn't keep up. With thirty minutes to class, I hit the student union to get caffeinated. The funky little cafe had been the landing place for Jade, River, and me when we started work at Concierge Services. Our weekly meetings were what kept us sane.

The coffee was hot, and as it cooled, I looked around campus and watched the couples walking hand in hand. Happy. Content. In love. They flirted and giggled while I stared in envy. I'd never had that. Hell-bent on getting my degree, I'd given up relationships. When I started escorting, it wasn't possible. River became my friend and a surrogate girlfriend until she fell in love with one of her clients. Jade was pregnant with her second child and still living with her two men. Then River married Jonathan and had a little boy.

And here I was, still single and whipping my dick out for dollars. The bitterness of the coffee tamed the bitterness of my mood. Twelve more weeks and I'd never have to sell myself again.

The weight of my emotions, or maybe my backpack, slowed my pace to a crawl across campus. Professor Thieland was my favorite instructor and my graduate advisor. Twice a week I attended his commodities class. The Monday and Friday classes were the highlights of my week, but even the prospect of attending one of his lectures couldn't diminish the cloud hanging over my head.

The auditorium hummed with the quiet voices of at least fifty students. At the podium, a ZZ Top look-alike tapped at the microphone.

In the fourth row, I sat in my Hugo Boss suit and waited. Did we have a guest speaker? The screech of audio feedback silenced the room.

"Good morning." The high-pitched voice of the man at the mike didn't mesh with the man in the Grateful Dead T-shirt and ratty jeans. "I'm Professor Saunders, and you've got me for the rest of the semester." Groans echoed through the lecture hall. "Jack Thieland had a family emergency and will be taking a sabbatical until next year. Keep him in your thoughts. This is Commodities in the Twenty-First Century, and I'll be using the synopsis and following the same curriculum of the class."

What else could go wrong? The last thing I needed at the eleventh hour was change. I pulled a paper out of my notebook and wrote 'screw me' over and over again. I wanted to scream it, but writing it in big bold letters with exclamation points seemed my best option. I crumbled the paper up and set the balled up page in the cup holder beside me.

A slim and sexy little brunette stood beside Professor Saunders. She was good-looking, curved in all the right places with long, shiny dark hair and eyes the color of sapphires. She handed him a few notes and stepped away. I watched her walk off the stage and take a seat at a makeshift desk set up to his right. She puckered her lips and blew at the hair that had fallen across her face. She appeared as happy as I felt.

"Twelve of you are graduate students and owe me a graduate project. Be patient as we try to squeeze you into my schedule. My assistant, Mim, will be here after class to talk to those of you who have already scheduled their presentations." He picked up a remote control and turned on the overhead projector for his lecture. "This is not an ideal situation for any of us, but like the stock market, there are highs and lows, and those who fare the best know how to ride the wave."

The rest of class slipped by in a haze. I was preoccupied with thoughts of work and mesmerized by Mim. Something about her drew me in. I didn't know if it was the way her hair flowed over her shoulders and curled on top of her breasts, or if it was the way the light bounced off her blue eyes. I'd been a point A to point B guy for so long, I'd never noticed anything else along the journey, but Mim could not be overlooked.

Class dismissed, I made my way to the table.

"Name?" she asked without looking up.

"Hi." One word was all I spoke. I wanted her to look up at me so I could lose myself in her eyes.

"Name?" she said again, with more than a hint of impatience.

"Hi," I repeated. "I know you're busy, but there's no need for bad manners. Mim, is it?"

She lifted her eyes from the paper and placed her pen to the side. "I'm sorry. This…" she spread her hands on the table, "was not what I had planned today. Yes, it's Mim, like Mom with an I." She let out a sigh.

Her English accent took me by surprise. "Well, Mom with an I, life has a way of throwing you curve balls at the least opportune times. I'm Luca Gregorio by the way."

I held out my hand, and she gently placed the tips of her fingers in my palm. I should have shaken her hand and dropped it, but being the suave Italian I was, I lifted her fingers to my lips and hovered over her knuckles. The roll of her eyes wasn't what I expected, nor was the snap of her hand like I'd burned her with my touch.

"Does that work for other girls?" She picked up her pen and scrolled down the names on her list. "Are You Getting What You Pay For? Commodities in the twenty-first century?" She recited my project title like it was an offering on the menu of a low-end diner.

"Yep, it generally works, and yep, that's me." I squatted down so we were at the same level. Eye level. When our gazes connected, I would have sworn I saw a glimmer of something other than impatience. Mim was a tough sell but hey this was my field of study.

"May ninth at two o'clock." Her voice was direct leaving no room for negotiation.

"What? No. That's three weeks earlier than I planned." Holy hell, how was I supposed to meet that deadline?

"You heard the professor. Those who do the best are those who learn how to ride the wave."

"This isn't a wave. It's a damn tsunami."

She wrote the date and time on a sticky note and handed it to me. With a tilt of her head and a smile on her face, she said, "There's no need to be rude." She looked past me to the woman standing behind me. "Next."

Speechless, I stormed out of the auditorium and went directly to the gym. The only work I'd put into my project was picking out the title. Unless I dropped everything, getting it done was a long shot. I rolled my shoulders, but the tension wouldn't ease. The only way to get rid of my stress was to sweat it out. I had three hours until my next appointment. Two would be spent working myself into a state of exhaustion.

The Athletic Club was a perk of working for Concierge Services I'd lose soon. Jack, my trainer, was by the weights when I arrived.

"Luca, what are we doing today?" He was always in high spirits, and I wondered if he got off torturing people. I worked out all the time. It was the only way to maintain the body my clients expected, and the added benefit was stress relief.

"Work me hard," I told him. "I've had a shit day." I changed into shorts and a cotton tee and met Jack at the weights. Bench-pressing my max for three sets would help right things in my twisted world for the moment.

One-press

Two-press

Three-press …

After three sets, I rose from the bench and bent over to hold my knees. I was pumped to continue once I caught my breath.

"Give me thirty minutes on the elliptical. I want it set to cardio, raise the resistance and the incline." Jack pushed me toward the machines and walked away.

The only machine available sat between a female with a sweet ass, and a fat dude with a visible plumbers crack. I climbed aboard and began. A glance to my left, and I nearly fell off.

"Not so smooth now, are you?" Mim pulled the handles and pressed the pedals like a pro.

What could I say? My swag factor had hit a low. "I'll get it together, don't worry about me."

"I'm hardly worried, Luca."

She remembered my name. That had to be good, right? Not wanting to be outdone. I upped my speed, resistance, and incline to match hers. Game on. "Odd that we would meet here. There have to be hundreds of gyms in the city." I huffed out the words. Cardio wasn't my thing. I did it to gain endurance, but now that I was at the end of my tenure with Concierge Services, I'd be able to cut back.

"It's the best, and I like quality." Her eyes ran the length of my body.

"Like what you see?" I tightened my hands on the grips so every muscle in my arms would bulge with definition.

"I love muscle. It's a damn shame most of yours seems trapped in your head. Inflated ego much?" She stopped her machine and hopped off.

"Hey, you've got me all wrong." I stepped off and followed her closely.

"Prove me wrong, Luca. Buy me a drink. I'll be at the coffee bar in ten minutes." She disappeared into the women's locker room before I could reply.

Shit. I had the time, but what was the point? *The point was, I wanted a distraction from my life, and she was hotter than hell.* I raced to the locker room and showered. I ran in the direction of the coffee bar with my tie in my hand. Nine minutes had passed, and I didn't want to miss the opportunity to get to know the brown-haired girl who had gemstones for eyes.

Dressed in an off-the-shoulder white tunic and black yoga pants—*God, I loved yoga pants*—she sat at the counter and watched me cross the floor toward her. I slid onto the stool beside her.

"What can I get you?" I waved the barista over and waited while Mim decided what she wanted.

"Chai tea with honey, please." She was all sweetness and sunshine to the tired-looking barista.

She was vinegar and hot sauce to me, but I liked flavor in my life. Mim intrigued me. "Double shot latte, please." I pulled my tie over my head and proceeded to finish dressing.

"That much caffeine will keep you up all night."

"Would seem that I'll need it. I have a project to finish three weeks early." I pulled a napkin from the dispenser and folded it in half.

Her smile didn't reach her eyes, but her lips twisted in a satisfied grin. "That's a shame."

The barista placed our drinks on the counter in front of us.

"Definitely."

"Will that cut into your social life?" She pulled the cup to her mouth and blew on the steaming liquid. I could smell the spice in her tea waft through the air.

"Are you asking out of interest?" *What was her game?* I was so out of the dating scene. I had no idea how women my age behaved.

"Possibly."

"I thought my ego offended you." I wasn't used to people casting me aside and pulling me back. She was playing me well.

"Your ego arouses my curiosity. I'd love to see what holds that up."

'Arouse' was an interesting word to use when talking about my self-esteem. "I'm told it's my incredible traps." I flexed my muscles to make a point.

She tried to suppress her laugh but ended up bursting out loud. "No wonder you work out. It must take a lot of muscles to hold up your head."

"Now you're just being mean, but I'll forgive you if you have dinner with me." *What the hell was I doing?*

She pulled my folded napkin from under my cup, took a pen from her backpack and wrote her address on it. "I'm free next Thursday. Seven works for me. I like Italian." She checked me out again before she rose from her seat and walked away.

I sat there, dumbfounded. I had a Thursday date with a frustrating woman who apparently liked Italian. That was one area in which I could deliver. A slow smile spread across my face.

———

THE SATURDAY NIGHT crazies were swarming Times Square by the time the cab dropped me off at the hotel. I was never late to an appointment, although I'd come close yesterday when an accident in the subway delayed me by an hour. Today, I'd started out early. I picked up the key to Claire's hotel room with plenty of time to spare.

I'd let myself into the room decorated in various shades of white. The purity of the color contrasted with the darkness of my soul. Life had become blurred. The only difference between a porn star and me was a porn star got paid to get laid on camera. I got paid to satisfy women. I didn't allow cameras. Voyeurism wasn't my thing.

After a glance around the suite, I knew Claire would want to be had on every surface in this room. The bed, the sofa, the tub, and the damn granite counter of the bar. My dick would be on fire before the evening was over.

The windows beckoned with the bright light of Times

Square flashing before me. I yanked the curtains closed, shutting out the real world around me while I produced one client's fantasy.

After a call to room service, I set about earning my pay. Claire had specifics she liked ready when she arrived. The tub had to be filled with hot water and bubbles. The champagne chilled in a silver bucket by the bed. I started the bath, lit the candles, and prepared the items she'd had delivered. When I took the lid off the box left behind, I wanted to scream. I hated this stupid fetish of hers. There were cuffs and a flogger, a handful of hundreds, and a brand new package of condoms.

I knew how this would play out. I'd answer the door in my thousand-dollar suit, and she'd pretend she was the escort. She'd show up in a trench coat with little or nothing beneath it. I'd sweet talk her into taking a bath where she would make me watch her masturbate. Priming herself was what she called it, but all it did was make the second orgasm much harder for her to reach. It lengthened the game I wanted to shorten.

I'd pretend to pay her, and she would tie me up and have her way. In any other setting it could be considered rape, but in this setting it was prostitution. I would sell myself once again to reach my goals: success, financial freedom, and respect.

When the knock came, I checked myself in the mirror. I ran my fingers through my hair, giving it what Claire would call a mussed up, sexy look. Making her wait was part of the game, so I straightened my tie and picked lint off my collar until the second knock sounded. It would annoy her to have to wait, but she got off on pent-up frustration. I rubbed the exhaustion from my eyes and prepped for the long night ahead. I tucked my self-loathing away and put on my Ken doll smile. *Showtime.*

I opened the door in a coat and dagger fashion, a sliver at a time. It added to her excitement. "Are you the girl?" I deepened my voice because she loved it. A baritone voice would earn me a sizable tip.

"Yes, I'm what you wanted," her words breathy and soft. So unlike the powerhouse of a woman I knew her to be. She was a CEO at Evictus Financial Group, a large firm specializing in penny stocks. I always gave Claire what she wanted because she had what I needed—money and a foot in the door at her company.

"You are indeed what I ordered." I ran my hand down her cheek. "Stunning." I pulled her into the room and peeked out the door as if someone could be watching. I had to play my part to perfection.

I'd been screwing my way into the door of Evictus for eighteen months now. A year and a half was a long time to be with the same client. She was one of my first, and we had this date every Saturday night like clockwork. Different hotel. Same situation. I'd pound her flesh so she'd be sore until our next date. She'd pay me and often press a generous tip in my pocket. In turn, I'd pay my rent, buy my groceries, and chip at my student loans. It was a living, but hardly a life.

For a second, I thought of Mim and locked the thought away behind my smile. She wasn't part of this world, and I wouldn't dirty her by thinking about her while I was on the job.

"Don't forget," said Claire. "I get paid up front." Yep, she always did, and she'd turn around later and hand over the cash for a night well spent.

I pulled out the bills I'd put in my wallet. Two circular divots marred the inside pocket. One came from the MBA coin my favorite professor gave me when I was struggling to pass my classes. "Keep your eye on the prize," he told me, and I've kept the talisman in my pocket ever since. The second circle used to contain my Saint Christopher, but now the space was empty. I had taken it out and put it in my drawer. I didn't need a daily reminder of how far I'd fallen.

I fanned the bills in front of her. "This should take care of it." I folded the wad of bills and placed them in her coat pocket. *Let the games begin.* With a firm tug, I pulled the belt of the coat loose and let it fall open. Hmm, black lingerie tonight. She must have had a terrible week. Anxiety slithered up my spine, wrapped around my neck and threatened to choke me. If her mood was dark, she'd want it rough and hard, which meant she'd give my body no mercy.

"What should I call you?"

"Call me Claire." The use of her real name was a surprise. She dropped the coat on the floor and pushed her body against me. For a woman in her forties, she had a rockin' body, but I was pretty sure it was because she devoured lesser men for sport.

"Well, Claire, I've prepared a bath for you. Climb in while I get you a drink." She turned toward the bathroom and walked away, exaggerating the sway of her hips. I knew she'd turn around and expect me to be watching her. I stayed and stared, and she looked over her shoulder and smiled. She was pleased, and that would earn me another bonus.

When I entered the bathroom, she was tucked neck deep in the water with her hair pulled up in a clip. The light of the candles flickered across the bubbles, creating a kaleidoscope of colors.

"Champagne?" I offered her a filled flute.

"No, you drink the bubbly. Tonight, I need something stronger. I'd prefer scotch." Her jade green eyes had turned the color of beached seaweed. Something was up. She was a creature of habit, and this wasn't our usual routine. "Get me a real drink."

What the hell was going on?

If I asked her, the fantasy would be ruined. I couldn't afford for that to happen. I needed tonight's gig for my rent, so I buried my questions and did as I was asked.

When I returned to the bathroom, she had her knees pulled up to her chest and was crying. "Tears?" The scotch sloshed back and forth from my unsteady hand. "What can I do?" I wasn't prepped for this. I was hardwired to avoid emotion since the day I began this job.

"Take off your clothes and get in the bath." Her voice cracked ever so slightly. Whatever was happening, she was clutching the ledge with her fingers, causing the tips to turn white.

Moisture had affected her mascara, making the black gel run into the fine lines on her face. Typically so put together,

Claire seemed a bit worn tonight, and that made her look vulnerable and soft—a side I'd never seen from this woman. We didn't share love or affection, but we had a mutual respect for one another.

I wanted to reach out and comfort her, and that scared me. "I don't think so, I hired you." It was important for me to get back on script. "I want you bathed, naked, and in bed in ten minutes." Pivoting on my heels, I exited the bathroom.

Her scream followed me into the bedroom. "Forget the script! I need to be held and comforted. Earn your money, Luca, and get your ass in here."

Rage surged through me. When I sold my body, it came with a bit of my soul attached. I felt thin, stretched out, and so very cold. My teeth ground until my jaw hurt. It was the only way to hold in the anger.

Since the Dom Perignon was mine alone, I pulled it from the bucket and guzzled straight from the bottle. Something told me things were about to change, and I'd need the 12.5% alcohol by volume to survive the night. Hell, I might need Claire's scotch to make it through the next hour.

I walked back into the bathroom, tugging at the tie Claire had given me last month. The Windsor knot of the blue silk tie nearly choked me. Whoever said fake it until you make it must have worked on Wall Street. Every day I showed up to work, I prayed it would be my last, but the reality was, I knew I'd keep doing this until my goals were met.

Claire's eyes dimmed, and I suppressed the panic that inched up my throat to gag me.

"Get in the tub, Luca." She tipped the scotch glass back and emptied the tumbler. "Refill first." The crystal glass screeched as she pushed it across the marble surround of the tub.

This was my life. She called, and I came. She demanded, and I delivered. She paid, and I performed. Rather than pour two fingers of scotch, I poured four to avoid another trip to the decanter. Despite wanting to drown myself in alcohol, I abstained. One of us had to be in control.

I transferred the glass to her hand and began the slow process of removing my suit. She needed comfort, and I needed money. With sixty thousand dollars remaining on my student loan, I couldn't take my eye off the goal.

I slid into the hot bubbles and situated myself across from her. I left the foil condom wrapper in clear view so there was no doubt where me, naked, and in the bathtub, would lead. She cupped the amber liquid with both hands and watched me over the rim.

Like a cat being stalked by a mouse, my internal protection mechanisms screamed for me to escape and evade, but I planted my ass and held my ground. For enough money, I'd ignore the warnings.

"Do you want to talk?"

My relationship with her was unique. She never shared personal information, which was probably why this arrangement had lasted so long. We weren't friends. Once all the bells and whistles were removed, I was simply a dick for hire, and she was a checkbook and a reference letter. For fourteen hundred dollars a night, I'd suffer through it.

"No." She stretched her foot out and rubbed her toes between my legs.

Habit required I make a sound of satisfaction. "Mmm," came from my mouth without thought or feeling. It was amazing how much a body could do on autopilot.

"Feel good?"

"It always feels good."

Slow, steady breaths helped me get my head in the game. I was like Pavlov's dog. In the zone, I could perform without thinking. When thrown off my game, it took a lot of coaxing. Tonight, I was out of my element.

Below the bubbles, I massaged her foot with one hand and my dick with the other. Once hard, I pulled her body toward me and set her between my thighs.

"What do you want, Claire?" The question was asked out of courtesy. This woman was a whip-wielding rough rider. She was a take-no-prisoners client. I imagined she operated much the same way in the boardroom as she did in the bedroom.

"I want to feel wanted." Her usually demanding voice diminished with each word. "I want to feel valued." Her shoulders rolled forward. "I want you to take charge."

Whoa. "What the hell is going on here? If you want to change the dynamics of our relationship, I need to know the new rules." This dicking around was driving me crazy.

"I was fired today."

Her body shook, and sobs escaped.

"What the hell?"

The air was sucked from my lungs. Although I was head

and shoulders above the bubbles, I was drowning under the weight of what her statement meant. All my eggs were in her basket. I'd nourished this relationship, made it a priority because making her happy gave me what I needed. Now, after eighteen months of letting her use me and control me, I was no closer to getting what I wanted. Eighteen damn months of whips and cuffs for nothing. Despair made me go limp. I threw my head back and stared at the ceiling.

"I don't want to talk about it. I want to forget about it."

She turned around and straddled me. She squeezed and pulled at my flesh, but there was no way my flaccid penis would rise to the occasion. My libido had sunk as low as my hope.

After several minutes, she gave up and collapsed back into the water.

Chapter 2

She shook in my arms in spite of the warm water that covered us. I struggled to gain my footing.

"Let me help you up."

Dripping with water and angst, I helped her up and over the tub ledge, following right behind her. She stood shivering with her arms covering her breasts. The bath bar cried out in protest when I dragged the towel from it. The soft cotton wrapped twice around her body.

She lifted the tail of the towel and dabbed at her eyes. When I saw she had missed some of the black that had stained her cheek, I pulled the edge of the towel up and wiped it away. Claire was my cash cow. With her as a regular, I didn't have to court any other overnights. At three hundred fifty dollars an hour, I pulled in an additional fourteen hundred a week with four other clients. All regulars, with lesser needs than her.

The prospect of having to bring in a new client so close to the finish line made my stomach coil with revulsion. What would I have to subject myself to in order to meet my goals?

"I got it," she said as she yanked the corner of the towel from my grasp and turned toward the door. She was a certifiable mess, and for the first time in a year and a half, I felt something other than indifference.

She turned and walked out of the bathroom, leaving me to ponder those thoughts. I didn't have time to get sentimental. I needed a new plan and quick.

With a towel wrapped around my waist, I entered the bedroom to find her curled in a ball on the bed. Did I get dressed and leave, or stay and offer comfort?

"Claire?"

"Hmm?"

She didn't move, so I sat beside her. My hands felt foreign to me as I brushed the hair from her face. "What can I do? Do you want me to stay or leave?"

"Do what you want, Luca. I'll pay you for tonight regardless." She pulled up the sheet and rubbed at her eyes.

My heart took off at a sprint that my legs begged to follow, but I squelched the urge to run. I didn't recognize the woman in front of me. Gone was Attila the Honey, and in her place was a broken woman who needed something. What that something was, I had no idea, but I'd dig deep to find it. I owed her that much.

When I climbed into bed beside her, she curled into my body and cried. Her warm salty tears spilled down my bare chest and seeped into my heart. I stroked her back and her body until her sobs became sighs, and to my shock, I became hard. Rock hard for her without putting my head in the zone. I'd let go of the stress of performance and let my body take over. What the hell was happening to me? She had to feel me. I was pressed firmly against her stomach.

She slipped her hand between our bodies and softly stroked me. Claire wasn't soft about anything, and the sensation nearly undid me.

"Luca, I want to give you something tonight. This meeting will be our last for a while, maybe forever, and I owe you so much."

She rolled me back and edged between my legs. Claire took, not gave. She was hard, not soft. I was confused, and my body had no idea how to respond until she wrapped her lips around my length and let her tongue stroke every stiff inch of me.

Fear, shame, and passion assaulted me, and I was unable to handle the emotions, so my mind shut down, and all I could do was feel. I closed my eyes and took what she offered. With infinite care and patience, she licked and laved at me until my body shuddered, and I spilled into her warm, velvet, mouth. Nothing had felt that intense in years. My heart gripped with emotions that had been buried since my first paycheck from Concierge Services.

Claire crept up my body and laid her head on my chest. "I'm going to miss you, Luca. I hope you'll miss me for more than my money."

I pulled her up over me and wrapped my arms around her. I didn't know what to say, so I said nothing at all.

WE SAT AT THE TABLE, eating breakfast. Normally I was out the door long before the sun rose, but today was different. The weight of the world rested on my shoulders, and I wasn't in a hurry to tackle the day. I'd taken a break last night and let life take the driver's seat, but as soon as I walked out of this room, I would need to steer.

"Make sure you fill out your invoice for me." Claire sipped at her espresso and scoured the New York Times.

"Are you sure? I don't want to charge you when you didn't get what you wanted." My bacon crumbled and fell to my lap. I had dressed in the jeans I had brought with me. Wearing a suit on Sunday brought back too many memories of church and family.

"Sometimes what we want doesn't always mesh with what we need, Luca. You gave me what I needed last night. You gave me your time, your patience, and your compassion." She reached across the table, and in a familiar touch, she gripped my hand. "I needed that."

I rose to gather my things. This moment felt very similar to the last day of high school, when I left so many people I'd spent years with but hardly knew. They were familiar and comfortable, and when I left them, it was foreign—scary.

She rose from her seat and pressed a wad of hundred dollar bills in my hand, along with her personal business card. After a year and a half, she was giving me her cell phone number. "Call me when you need that reference letter.

I'd be happy to write one for you." She leaned into my chest, and I pressed a kiss to the top of her head.

"I will." I tucked the money and the card into my pocket. "What will you do now?"

"Oh…there's a company in Chicago that's been trying to recruit me for years. I think I may take them up on their last offer. Maybe I'll meet someone and fall in love." Wistfulness filled her voice.

"Chicago is a beautiful city. It has a lot to offer you, and you have a lot to offer as well. Don't forget that." To say it was a small world was an understatement. What were the chances she'd end up at the place I had to escape? She would find her future and freedom in the one place that tried to harness and control mine.

A smile danced on her lips. "Too bad you're twenty years too young for me. Luca, find a girl your age, fall in love, get married, and grab the world by the balls." She looked around the hotel room. "You deserve more than this." She lifted up onto her tiptoes to place a kiss close to my lips. It felt odd at first because we had never kissed. In fact, kissing was more intimate than intercourse. I'd had sex with lots of women, but I'd never kissed one of them for money.

I swung the garment bag over my shoulder and walked out the door. My life had changed drastically in a single breath. Yesterday I had a three-month plan to financial freedom, and now I'd be back to eating Ramen and turkey dogs.

I swallowed my panic. Calm was a requirement in dire circumstances.

Rather than take the subway, I walked the fifteen blocks

toward home. It would give me time to process everything that happened in the last day. Once I turned onto 46th Street, the sound of the pipe organ from St. Mary the Virgin Church echoed down the block. Like a mouse in search of cheese, I wandered in that direction until I found myself standing on the threshold of the church. A big sign out front said they were doing a fundraiser to pay for maintenance on the organ. My heart tingled at the thought of entering, but my feet wouldn't budge. I had visions of touching the holy water and bursting into flames.

"Come inside." The young priest held out his arm in welcome. "We welcome saints and sinners alike. Besides, the music sounds better when trapped by the walls and stained glass."

"No thanks, I'm fine here."

I leaned against a cement planter near the curb. Far enough away to feel like my presence didn't sully the parish, but close enough to soak in a tiny bit of grace, and the sound of an antique pipe organ.

I pulled the wad of hundreds from my pocket and began to straighten them out. Four of them, I tucked inside my wallet. Seeing the MBA coin hiding between two bills caused a stutter in my heart. I rubbed it for luck and tucked it back into my pocket. Instead of keeping my eye on the prize, I was watching it disappear. I snapped the two remaining bills open and tucked them into the priest's palm as I walked away. There wasn't enough money in the world to save me, but maybe it would be enough to keep the pipe organ playing a bit longer. As I walked away, I could hear it fading, like my hope of salvation.

When I finally entered the foyer of my apartment building, pallets of tile blocked my usual path. The old tile was homey and comforting with its cracks and worn finish. I counted the steps from one crack to the next. Life was like that, imperfect in a perfect way, but life changed, and so would the tile in the entry of my building. Nothing stayed the same.

Three flights up, I reached my flat. It wasn't much, but it was all my budget of eighteen hundred a month could afford. I jiggled the key until the lock gave way. Usually, I'd touch my fingers to my lips and press them to my wish wall as I passed.

I'd made the collage when I'd first started pimping myself for money. Staring at what hovered just out of reach, I ripped the poster board free from the wall and tore it to pieces, letting my dreams fall to the floor. My plan needed modification.

After tossing the garment bag on my unmade bed, I went in search of my black marker and ruler. My new circumstances called for creativity. I sat down to devise a backup plan. I was burning brain cells when my phone rang.

"Hey, Mom." I didn't have to look at the screen. She called every Sunday. In fact, I could set my clock by her call.

"Luca, did you go to church?" It was the first question out of her mouth every week.

"Yep, I stopped by this morning. The pipe organ was beautiful." It wasn't a lie entirely.

"Oh, cuore mio," she sang out. Apparently, I'd made her heart happy. She only spoke Italian when she was pissed or overjoyed. There was no way the term 'my heart' could mean anything but happiness. "Did you wear your suit?"

Again, I lied. "Yes, but I carried the jacket over my shoulder." *Along with my shirt and tie and pants.* I had a foot in Hell already, but surely God would give me some dispensation if my lies were intended to bring happiness to my mother. *Nah, probably not.*

"Sono tanto fiera di te," she bubbled as she told me how proud she was of me. Italian mothers never stopped worrying about their kids.

"When are you coming to see your mother?" She spoke in that direct, no-nonsense way only a mother of five boys could. "Mothers need to see their sons and know they are well. It's been too long since you've been home. Is Chicago that bad, or are you avoiding your parents?"

I silently blew air from my mouth and rolled my eyes. If she knew the truth, it would destroy her. My mother was incredibly perceptive, and face-to-face she'd see me for what I was—a man-whore.

"No, I'm busy with school and work." It was the first full truth I'd said all day. I was busy, and with the loss of Claire, my life would get busier. "I have three months to go, and then I'll come for a visit."

"You're breaking your mother's heart, Luca. I need to see you to know you are safe and well."

It was always Mom's desire to see me, but I wondered about my Dad. He rarely came on the phone.

"Soon, I promise. Soon."

We chatted for a few minutes, and she told me about the big feast they would enjoy as a family today. Every Sunday was the same, five courses and eating for hours on end. I felt bitterness at the word 'family'. I had ruined my parents' dream of having everyone live in Chicago and work in the family electrician business. I'd wanted something more—something different. When we hung up, I zoned out and thought about the conversation I'd had with my father the day I left for college.

"You disappoint me," he said. "You're wounding my heart. I built this for my boys." He pounded on his work van. Gregorio Electric stood out in bold, red letters on the side of the white panel. "You as the oldest were to take over and guide your brothers, but no, you want different. Aren't we good enough?"

"Dad, this isn't about you. It's about me being my own man. Making my way in the world. I don't want to be you. I want to be me."

I hated the electrician business. The money was decent, but the schedule was a grind. Your life belonged to the next call coming in. What was the crime in wanting more? I didn't want to be a carbon copy of my father. I wanted to earn more, be more, have more.

"You go to that fancy school in the city and get yourself in debt. I bet when you're finished, you won't make more than an electrician's apprentice."

He'd left me in the driveway to choke on his words.

Four years later, I walked across the stage with my diploma in my hand and a huge debt in my name. Dad had been right. The first company that offered me a job as a financial advisor intern offered less than Dad paid as an apprentice. So, I traveled far from my hometown of Chicago and enrolled in a master's degree program in New York, the center of the financial world. If I couldn't meet my goals here, I'd never be able to meet them. There was no way I would go home and admit defeat.

Chapter 3

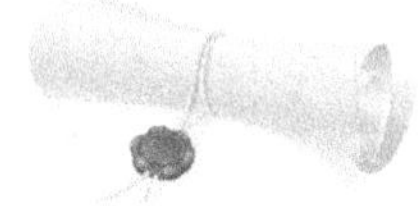

Sandra had built Concierge Services on a solid premise. Those in the biz called it The Dean's List since only the wealthy benefactors of the university were allowed to participate. I needed another wealthy patron. The rich bought what they wanted, and young coeds filled the need. For the right amount of money, any sexual fantasy could be fulfilled. The girls got the better end of the deal. Men were far more generous with their cash and gifts than women.

Female clients demanded so much more. They wanted the besotted boyfriend experience. I had to be sophisticated, sexy, well-mannered, a great dancer, a great listener, a fantastic lover, a hard body, a romantic, and a mind reader. In exchange, I was paid the fee. On occasion with some, and always with Claire, I earned a bonus and gifts. I had enough ties to open a store. I even scored a Tag Heuer watch last

Christmas. A gift from Claire for a year well spent. I would miss Claire.

Upon entering the office, the soft perfume of the receptionist floated through the air. Merilee wore a cotton candy scent that made me reminisce about amusement parks and childhood.

She'd been working here for as long as I had. "Hey, Merilee, she's expecting me." I walked to the right wall and pushed. The panel popped open, and I slipped into Sandra's lair. I'd spent more than my fair share of time here. The room was cold and sterile like the woman who occupied it. White furniture, dark woods. Dark and light. Black and white. No gray zone.

The last time I was here was because a client had attacked River. She left the service, but Sandra brought the rest of us in to discuss safety. It was the first time I'd seen the entire staff of only a handful of men and close to forty women.

The time before that, I had refused to let a client peg me, and I was brought in to discuss flexibility. I considered myself flexible but drew the line at women with strap-on dildos.

Today, I came on my own accord to solicit help. I was short by over four grand a month, and if I couldn't obtain my goal, I'd have to face my father and admit I'd failed. No way was that happening.

Sandra wielded control in everything, but I wasn't beyond sucking up a little to get what I needed. Everyone set their standards, and mine had plummeted to a new low.

She rose from her desk, dressed in a crisp black suit. Her

white shirt was starched so heavily, I feared it would crack. "You sounded disturbed when you called, Luca. What could be wrong with my hot Italian stud?" She pulled a tray of beverages from the side bar and walked to the white sofa to take a seat. The click of her black slingbacks snapped the silence like a whip.

Ever the obedient employee, I followed and sat in the chair beside her. "Claire was fired. I need to pick up three new clients for an hour a week or one overnighter."

"Claire called and resigned from the service this morning. I can see where that would be a problem for you."

"'Problem' is an understatement. I need the money she was providing. It's part of my long-term plan." The stress of the night gave me a kink in my neck. I rolled it around and heard the *pop, pop, pop* of the vertebrae falling into place. Maybe this situation was like a spine. It was out of alignment and needed manipulation to fall into place.

Sandra frowned. "You're on your last lap here, Luca. I don't know what you expect from me. Most clients don't want to purchase a new toy, only to have to return it within a few months. You know once you graduate, you can't stay. Those are the rules."

"I need a miracle, Sandra. I didn't sell myself for nearly two years to *almost* get there. Surely, there's someone who wants me short-term."

Never would I have guessed that three months before the end of my tenure at Concierge Services, I'd be benched. I leaned forward and placed my elbows on my knees. I'd been told that my blue eyes could melt hearts. I looked at Sandra and prayed I could thaw her ice long enough to cut me some slack.

Sandra popped the top of the diet soda and poured it into a lowball glass. The effervescence bubbled into the air above the crystal. "The problem, Luca, is desperation and discernment don't mix well. You have to choose. If you're truly intent on reaching your goal, you'll be flexible. I know two women who would be happy to take you." She leaned back and stretched out her long legs.

A sick feeling churned in my gut. There were only two women I'd ever refused to see. One insisted on strapping on and making me her bitch. I'd done a lot of things in the past two years that I'd take back, but I still refused to stoop that low.

The other was a native New Yorker, who broke through the glass ceiling of the financial world face first. Lined up next to the men in her company, she would be hard to pick out as a woman. Diane's suits came from the finest menswear shop in the city, and she had her hair cut at the barbershop downtown. It was questionable as to what body parts were in her trousers.

Something about our meet-and-greet made me wonder if I'd feel feminine next to her, and that didn't sit right with my ego, so I'd opted not to see her again. My choices were slim, almost virtually gone. Sandra was telling me I'd have to choose between the two.

"Have Diane call me to set up a date." I picked at the invisible lint on my pants, afraid to look at Sandra's smug expression. She'd been hounding me to take on Diane for months.

I clenched my teeth to battle the frustration that was building from deep inside. Heat from my anger burned low in my stomach until I felt the warmth of it hit my ears. "I have to go. I have class in an hour."

Sandra stood and walked me to the opening in the wall. "Stop acting like someone ripped the arm off your teddy bear, Luca. You're not a boy, buck up and act like a man. This is a business. Honestly, Diane can be instrumental in your future. Make nice-nice with her, and you may be able to write your own ticket." She dismissed me with a flick of her wrist.

WHEN I WALKED into Professor Saunders class, I took a seat up front and watched the door for Mim.

When she entered, she scanned the room, and as soon as she found me, she smiled. I paid no attention to the lecture. My attention was focused on her and the way she looked up from her papers and grinned. She rushed out before class ended, but I'd had my Mim fix, and I was happy.

I ARRIVED at Laura Prater's office with a little pep in my leather loafers. Laura was my Monday quickie. She liked sex against the window of her forty-second-floor mid-

Manhattan office building. In spite of her exhibitionist fetish, this assignment would be easy, and I needed a bit of easy today. Nothing had been status quo since Saturday.

I rode the elevator to her floor. Her secretary, Bonnie, sat at her desk, looking bored.

"She's ready for you." Bonnie thought we met for mentoring sessions each week. That was what the service called these little meetings, and in the grand scheme of things, they could be considered tutorial if the client chose to teach me something. What I'd learned from most of my clients was that women in positions of power were often lonely at the top, and I was the means through which they alleviated that top-level stress.

"Thanks." I walked through the door of her office and locked it behind me. Laura sat in a red leather chair in front of the window, dressed in a skirt and thigh high stockings—nothing else. Pictures of her with famous people covered the walls. Movie stars. Presidents. Industry icons. In the corner sat a telescope. I'd always wondered what she looked at through the lens. The skies lit up with the bright lights of the city at night, so stargazing was not an option.

We didn't talk much. She was always near naked and dripping wet when I arrived. She needed no priming, no foreplay. She wanted what she wanted. She liked me fast and hard.

With my hands in my pockets, I drifted toward the telescope. "I've always wondered why the telescope?" I looked through the lens and stepped back. In the scope was a man watching through binoculars. His trousers were at his ankles, and his dick was in his hand. I stumbled back and knocked a picture of Laura and the Pope off the wall.

She shook her head and tsked. "Some things are better left unknown, Luca."

"Who the hell is that?" I peeked through the telescope again. It was like a train wreck that couldn't be ignored. Through the lens, I saw the same man stroking himself. Laura pushed the scope to face the wall and pulled me toward her.

She took her position, always bent over the leather chair with her side facing the window. "That's my boyfriend. This," she waved her hands around, "is our thing. Mondays, he watches; Wednesdays, I watch. He's a member of the service, too." She talked like it was normal for a man to watch his girl get laid by someone else. My thoughts went straight to Mim, but I immediately shut them down.

"This whole time?" We'd had this Monday date for the last eight months or so. This job was a highlight of my week because it was so easy. Now I wasn't sure I'd get hard. Knowing some sick bastard was across the street getting off made me nauseous.

"Yes, now let's get busy. He's waiting." She turned around and reached for me. "Oh, for Christ's sake, Luca, really?"

She dropped to her knees and slid a condom on my limp dick, then pulled me into her mouth. I don't care how uninterested I thought I was. When a woman sucked me, things happened against my will. Moments later, I was pumping my way to three hundred and fifty dollars. All the while, my insides twisted with humiliation. I would have never sunk this low had I known, and now that I did, I didn't have much choice but to perform.

Wanting this over as soon as possible, I reached around and stroked her to climax while her breasts swayed to our movement. She threw her head back and groaned into the palm I'd placed over her mouth. There was no sense alerting Bonnie to our misdeeds.

Five minutes later, I was running down the stairs–forty-two flights of them. I took the long way home, needing to burn off the filth that branded my skin like a bad tattoo. It was early afternoon when I passed in front of the church. I stopped at the door and debated going in but changed my mind. I needed more than a conscience cleansing. I needed an exorcism. I shoved my hand into my pocket and felt the smooth side of my coin.

Keep your eye on the prize.

Just as I passed the massive oak doors, the priest summoned me.

"Excuse me?" He rushed behind me and tapped me on the shoulder. "I could use a hand with something. Can you spare a minute?" His eyes pleaded.

Filled with indecision, I looked at the priest and then over my shoulder at my escape route. In the end, I nodded. He grabbed my arm and guided me into the narthex of the church. It had been two years since I stepped foot into a place of worship, and being pulled in by a priest wasn't how I'd imagined my re-entry into the faith.

My heart thumped in the cage of my chest. The sculptures of saints looked down at me like they knew every single sin I'd committed.

"I'm in a bit of a hurry. What did you need?" I'd never had a panic attack, but if it felt like someone sitting on my chest while simultaneously strangling me, I was having a full-blown episode right now.

"You can take a few minutes to serve God. I'm Father Tim Tobin, and you're the young man with the hundred dollar bills." I followed him into a back room filled with flowers. "The Parker wedding was yesterday, and they wanted to donate the flowers to the Alzheimer's center. Some of these arrangements are too heavy for me to manage on my own."

"No problem, Father." It seemed odd to be calling a man a few years my senior 'Father'. At a glance, it was easy to tell we were opposites. He was blond. I was dark-haired. He was short. I was tall. He was celibate, and I wasn't.

"If we can load these into the van out back, that would be great." Father Tobin picked up one side of a large urn of flowers, and I picked up the other. "You walk past the church a lot, but you never come in. I'd love for you to join us at Mass. You can listen to the pipe organ you helped repair." We walked the flowers to the pristine white van and placed them inside.

"Thanks for the invite. I'll think about it." We loaded the remaining floral arrangements, and Father Tobin walked me back through the church.

He stopped me in front of the Pieta. "She was a perfect mother, and he was the perfect son. Her beautiful expression shows her resignation to his fate. She had the faith of a thousand."

I looked at Mary gazing upon her son with love. "Yes, she is perfect." Did every mother feel as passionate about her son as Mary had?

"There are many kinds of death. The one most beneficial is the death of sin. He died for yours." Father Tobin pointed to the confessional. "Let me hear your sins so you can bury them."

I shook my head. "Thanks for the offer, Father, but you have to be willing to stop the sin to bury it, and I'm not there yet." I brushed away the bead of sweat that fell across my brow and glanced back at the statue before I walked out.

By the time I made it home, I was exhausted and hungry. I buried my thoughts in a can of chili and a box of saltines while I watched a marathon of sitcoms and rubbed my MBA coin between my fingers. Just before bed, my phone buzzed with an incoming message from Sandra.

Luca,

Good news for you. I'm putting you on call. Don't say no, you asked for this. Wednesday night you're going to a fundraiser. Check your calendar.

Sandra.

Judith Kent was a new addition to my Wednesday calendar. Her biography listed her at eighty-four years old. *Holy crap.* She had no employment recorded, but it was obvious she had money. Her photo showed her dripping in diamonds. Thankfully, her bio said companionship only. I loved the no sex "dates". River had a no sex regular named

Ben. She loved him and continued to see him even after she left the service. God, I missed River.

Not willing to give up my Thursday time with Mim, I typed a message back to Sandra.

Sandra,

Not sure I like the idea of being "on call" and my new client is old enough to be my grandmother. Don't book me on Thursday because I have plans.

Luca

With Sandra, I had to be definitive. If I didn't give her parameters, she'd have me naked and working out of the back of a truck to accommodate her clientele.

Luca,

I'm nearly old enough to be your grandmother if your mother had you at ten. Don't forget you asked me to help you reach your goal. Surely you remember that saying about beggars and choosers. Get your tux ready and stop whining.

Sandra

For someone to tell me to stop whining was a first for me. I'd never been a complainer, and I'd never been a whiner, but getting this close and seeing my dream just out of reach was depressing. I'd managed to pay off over a hundred and fifty thousand dollars in student debt. I wasn't going to throw in the towel at the eleventh hour when things got sticky.

Tomorrow was Tuesday; coffee at the Student Union with River and Jade, then my math lab. Clients filled the afternoon. It was twofer Tuesday, Meredith Hostetter at seven, and Shelby Nivens at nine. Generally speaking, Wednesday would be my free day to catch up, but not this week. This week, I'd be escorting Judith Kent to what appeared to be a hospital fundraiser.

Maybe seeing Mim wasn't a good idea after all. Then again, I could use the distraction of Mim. I pulled my coin from my pocket. It glittered like the treasure it represented.

I WALKED into the coffee shop to find River and Jade at the same corner booth we'd been meeting at for as long as I could remember. We met through work, but our budding friendship held us together.

"Luca, you look like hell." Jade was always a tell-it-like-it-is girl. She sat next to River and stretched her legs under the table so her feet rested on my side of the booth. Her belly was already big, and she was just a few months along.

"Are you having twins?"

"Screw you." She flew me a double bird. Just goes to show you that being rich didn't guarantee decorum.

"It will cost you three hundred and fifty bucks, but I'm game if you are." I pulled off her shoes and rubbed her feet. I'd learned from both River and Jade that pregnant women always had sore feet.

She wiggled her toes in my hand. "I'd reach over and slap you if you weren't so good at rubbing my aching feet."

"You do look tired, Luca. What gives?" River was always

the empathetic one of the group. She was the perfect mother, friend, and mentor.

"Do you have a week? Let me get my coffee, and I'll tell you why this twenty-six-year-old looks and feels like he's forty." I gently put Jade's feet back down and went to get my regular bold brew. When I got back, River and Jade eyed me with concern.

Jade's lip twitched. "All right, spill." They both leaned into the center of the table where we divulged all secrets.

"Ms. Badass got fired, and so, in turn, I was let go." We always used code names. When River was seeing Jonathan before he became her husband, she called him Mr. Broom. We called Jade's men The Duo.

Both women gasped and said, "No," in unison.

"She's your number one. You were supposed to work for her. How in the hell does that happen?" River's face was ashen. She knew what that meant for me.

"It's not a situation I ever considered. Now I'm scrambling to make things work."

"Shit, Luca, that sucks. I can hire you to rub my feet until I pop out this next heathen." Jade rubbed her tummy. She talked tough, but she was an incredible mother. How she managed two men and her little girl Gabrielle, I had no idea.

"I may have to take you up on it. Do you think Eric and Todd will pay me three-fifty an hour to rub your toes?"

"Good luck with that." Jade pulled out her phone and began tapping at the keys. "The nanny wants to take Gabrielle to the park today. I'm just reminding her to bring sunscreen."

"Speaking of nannies, where's JJ?" River was rarely without her baby boy.

"He's with his daddy. Jonathan wanted to give me some time to feel like an ordinary person. Most days, JJ is attached to my boobs, but I pumped today. So I'm free for a few hours. I figured I'd see you and then get a pedicure."

"Look at you two. Too bad there's not a wealthy woman who wants to marry me and set me up for life." I glanced out the window and caught a glimpse of Mim walking across the campus. She appeared to be in a hurry. I watched her until she disappeared completely out of view.

"Earth to Luca." The kick to my shin brought me back to the coffee shop. "Who's that?" River asked.

"Did I tell you my favorite professor went on sabbatical, my graduate project is now due three weeks early, Sandra put me on call, I'm over fifty grand from my goal, and I met her?" I tossed my head in the direction Mim had disappeared. "She's the one."

"Who is she?" Jade asked.

"That's Mim." When I closed my eyes, I could see her smile and hear her laughter. "She's the assistant for my new professor. She's different. Bad attitude. Cute smile. Sexy accent."

River reached across and held my hand. "I'm so happy for you."

"It's not like that. I asked her to dinner, and she told me I was taking her out on Thursday. So now I have to decide if I'm going to show." Deep inside, I knew I'd go because even though Mim was frustrating in the few encounters I had with her, she was the most real thing I had right now besides these two.

Jade sat up and leaned in. "I call bullshit. You get a soft, warm look on your face when you say her name."

"She says she loves Italian." I bit my lip in that sexy way women liked and winked at my friends.

"Yes, but you can love Italian, or you can looove Italian. Which is it going to be?" River asked.

"I'm putting off the looove part," I said, mimicking River's drawn out word, "until I finish with the sex part." I picked at the side of my cup until I'd straightened the curled edge.

Jade leaned into the center of the table and gestured for us to join her. Her words weren't safe for all ears. "Screwing for money is way different from screwing for pleasure or love. When is the last time you had sex because you felt like it?"

"Too long." It was a simple and honest answer. I felt something with Claire the other night, but it wasn't love or affection. I wondered what it would feel like to bury myself in Mim. The thought gave me an immediate twitch in my dick.

River sat back, serious and contemplative. "You know, you don't have to finish to be a winner, Luca. There is no shame in coming out of college with some debt."

"I know, but that wasn't the plan. Besides, outside of the debt, I now have to get gainfully employed, and that's not going to be easy."

"Do you want me to talk to Jonathan? He might have a position open. I can also call Ben." River was a dreamer, full of hope and everything sweet. Jade was brutal reality, filled with tough love and hard truths. I was often the jokester, full of shit. That's why it worked for us. We all brought something to the table beside secrets.

"Let me see what I can work myself. Hell, I'm seeing the Face First client starting on Saturday. She's my new norm for the next twelve weeks."

Jade choked on her coffee. "No way." I'd told them about her last year when I'd first met Diane. "At least, you can find out who her tailor is."

"Don't be mean." River looked at Jade and scowled. "Do you remember the guy with the button for a penis?"

Jade and I nodded.

"He was the nicest man, and we learned a lot about each other in a short period. Luca, I'm going to challenge you to make her feel like a beautiful woman. In return, you might see her as one."

We finished our conversation with pictures of the babies and hugs all around. Our meetings had become less frequent since they had married, but it was those meetings that reminded me how lucky I was to call them friends.

———

I RAN off to class and then rushed home to get ready for my clients.

I met Meredith at her house. She always offered me a cocktail, but I always declined. I had Shelby right after her, so it wouldn't serve me well to get drunk.

Meredith was pretty. She was pushing mid-forties, and she was single. I imagine that all boiled down to the fact that she didn't like dick. She was oral all the way. The good thing was, I didn't need to be in the mood; I just needed to go through the motions. This client felt most like an ordinary job. I showed up, I did my job, and I left. Easy as that.

"Meredith, you look beautiful tonight."

She did; her red hair flowed down her back, and her wide hips swayed as she walked me into her bedroom. The jade green spread was new and looked lovely against her alabaster white skin.

"Thank you, Luca, I hope your day went well." Little did she know, today had been my best all week. I was ready to pleasure her.

"It's better now that I'm here." My head was in the game. My new mantra was *one lick, one dick, one tick off my list, and another day done.* "Do you want to hug and cuddle or just get down to business?"

She looked at the clock on her nightstand. "Let's get to it. I'm a bit tired tonight."

She reached into her drawer and pulled out the thin rubber dam we used as a barrier. I hated the taste of them, but precautions were needed when you worked in the sex trade. I pulled off my gray pinstriped jacket and laid it over the beige upholstered chair that sat next to the bed. Slowly and seductively, I peeled her pants and underwear from her body. She was bare from the waist down. I ran my fingertips up her legs and drew them across her stomach. Her muscles tensed under my touch. I typically didn't remove her shirt.

She'd never requested it, but tonight I wanted her to experience something different.

"What are you doing, Luca?" she asked as I pulled her top over her head. Her full breasts spilled over the edge of her bra.

"Something different. I want you to feel good and loved when I tuck you in tonight."

What was I doing?

River's comment about making Diane feel like a woman hit home. I'd been doing less of that lately with all of my clients, and so tonight I would start again with Meredith.

"Hmm," she hummed when I released the front snap and let her heavy breasts fall into my palms. "Why now?"

"Why not?" For some inexplicable reason, I wanted to give her more. If there was one thing I was an expert at, it was a woman's body. I'd had enough of them over the last two years to make me a specialist.

I focused on the rosy buds that had puckered to attention and ran the heat of my tongue over them until she squirmed across the bed. Her breath was labored, and she gripped handfuls of the comforter with each inhale. I sank to my knees, pulled the thin almost nothing rubber dam over her sex and focused my attention on her pleasure. Within minutes, she was shuddering and moaning, and I was pleased with myself. Pride in workmanship was something Dad had pounded into me. I wonder if he'd be proud of me now?

After a hug goodbye, I worked my way across town to Shelby. We had dinner and then a quickie in her car. I don't make the rules, I just follow directions—mostly.

―――――――――

Chapter 4

―――――――――

I saw Mim twice before school let out for the day. Once walking away from me, and once running to the financial aid building. I thought about running to catch up with her, but I wanted to savor her like a fine wine, so I just leaned against a tree and watched her. She ran with purpose, arms and feet pumping like she was on a machine at the gym, her hair blew in the breeze behind her. I closed my eyes briefly to capture the moment, and when I opened them again, she had disappeared into the building. I pushed off the tree and headed home to get ready for my date with Judith.

―――――――――

"JUDITH, I'M LUCA." The older woman stepped out of the limousine draped in sapphires and diamonds. "I'm your escort for the night." With her arm tucked in mine, we walked into the Marriott Marquis.

"Sandra was right. You are a treat to the eyes." She gripped my elbow. "A little candy for my arm." Up ahead, the elevators waited to whisk us to the event.

The ballroom was full of people whose pockets were full of money. Someone was getting fleeced tonight.

"What are we here for?" I pulled two glasses of champagne from the tray of a passing waiter and handed one to my past-her-prime date. She pinched her lips together and sipped at the bubbling liquid in the crystal fluted glass. More of her orange lipstick stayed on the glass than on her lips.

"We're here for a fundraiser for a new wing at the hospital. I'd love to have a wing named after me." She stopped, handed her glass to me and spread her hands in front of us both like she was unveiling something. "The Kent Center for Reproductive Health has a nice ring to it, doesn't it?"

"Yes." Good reproductive health generally led to kids. "Do you have children?"

She took back her glass and emptied the contents in one gulp. "No." The word spat out of her mouth.

"Oh, I'm sorry." She obviously wasn't able to have children, and I'd touched on a taboo subject.

"No reason to be. I never wanted children, so I opted not to have them. In my day, you were supposed to get married and have a handful of children, but diapers and bottles never appealed to me. I wanted a boardroom, not a nursery." Her voice held no regret. "Besides, I can rent whatever I need."

She straightened my bowtie and grinned. "Now smile and look handsome, Luca."

"Who will people think I am to you?" I rolled my lips into a Hollywood smile.

"Who cares? I just love for them to wonder. Let's keep them guessing." We walked up to the man in the center.

He had familiar blue eyes, but I knew I'd never met him. I always remembered names and faces, and despite his eyes seeming familiar, the rest of him drew a blank.

"Judith, you came. I can always count on you for support." The man leaned in and kissed both of Judith's wrinkled cheeks in a warm, friendly manner. "I see you brought a toy." He raised his brows in a you-can't-fool-me manner.

Offering my hand, I said, "I'm Luca Gregorio." The man widened his eyes at the mention of my name. "It's a pleasure to meet you." I waited for him to introduce himself, but he didn't. He pinched his lips between his fingers and stared.

Judith broke the silence. "This is Marcus Knight. He's the reproductive specialist raising money for the new wing. Be a dear and get me a scotch on the rocks, will you?"

I nodded to Judith, then to Marcus before I went in search of the bar. Looking over my shoulder, Marcus Knight never took his eyes off me.

The line at the bar was ten deep and moving at a slug's pace when a tap on my shoulder drew my attention.

"Hey stranger, I didn't expect to see you here."

Mim stood in front of me, looking like she'd stepped out of a fashion spread. Before working as an escort, I wouldn't have been able to distinguish between Prada and a chain store brand, but now I could pick out couture from crap at a glance. It was training that came in handy when you courted high-end women.

"Is that Prada?" I touched the soft fabric on the shoulder of her black and white cropped jacket. "It's very Jackie-O."

"Yes, it is Prada. Should I be concerned that you know that?" She reached up and tugged my black bowtie to the right. "Most men couldn't pick Prada from The Gap."

"I have an appreciation for a finely dressed woman." I stood back and took her in. I'd only seen her in slacks and yoga pants, but in her above the knee, hounds-tooth skirt, her legs took my breath away. All of that work on the elliptical certainly paid off.

Mim looked past me toward where I'd left Judith talking to Mr. Knight. "I saw you arrive with an older woman. Is she your grandmother?"

How could I explain Judith to her?

"Something like that." I hoped my vague answer would suffice. How could I tell the woman I was attracted to that I sold myself for cash? I couldn't, so I'd leave it vague.

"What does that mean?"

Shit. I should have known ambiguity wasn't going to fly with someone like Mim. She proved herself formidable when she boldly told me we were going out on Thursday. She was someone who got what she wanted, and for some crazy reason, she wanted me.

"She's a friend of a friend who needed a plus one for the night. I stepped in when she asked." Finally, at the bar, I ordered Judith's scotch on the rocks and a diet soda for myself. "Can I get you a drink?"

Mim nodded and asked for a glass of white wine, then followed me to where Judith was in deep conversation with Mr. Knight.

"Hi, Daddy." Mim leaned into Mr. Knight's side and kissed him on the cheek. "This is Luca, the man I have a date with on Thursday." Mim smiled up at her father.

My hand shook as I gave Judith her drink. What were the odds that I'd run into her dad? Judith grinned and began to laugh. Marcus scowled.

"She could do worse, Marcus. I can tell you his manners are impeccable."

Judith sipped her scotch as if nothing was happening, but something huge had occurred. Mim's father knew what I was, and by his scowl, he didn't approve. Marcus had referred to me as a toy, and he wasn't too far off the mark. I was a plaything for wealthy women.

"Miriam, can you take Judith to the model of the wing? Luca and I will join you in a moment."

Miriam? Was that the long form of Mim?

Marcus slapped his hand on my back. It was man language for *follow me, son, or suffer the consequences.*

Mim wrapped her arm through Judith's. "Be nice to him, Daddy. I'd like to get through the first date before you run him off." Her giggle floated through the air while she walked away.

Once the women were out of earshot, Marcus let loose

on me. "You will cancel your date with my daughter. She deserves more than a gigolo."

"Yes, she probably does, but I like her, and I haven't liked anyone since I started hating myself two years ago." It was the truth, and he needed to hear it because, in spite of the fact that I didn't deserve Mim, she made me feel a potent combination of irritation and desire, and I wanted to investigate where it could lead. "What I do is not who I am." I looked around the room to make sure no one could hear me. "I'm the oldest of five boys. I'm a son, a brother, a student, and yes, I sell my time. I'm not proud of what I do. It's a means to an end, and it will end—soon. Haven't you ever had to do something you weren't proud of because it was the best option at the time? This lifestyle wasn't an easy choice, but at the time it was the only option."

"I can't tell my daughter who to date or who not to. She is a stubborn woman. In fact, if I told her to drop you, she'd probably rush to the nearest chapel to marry you. I'm simply going to warn you. You do anything to hurt my daughter, and I'll shove your dick so far inside of you, no one will take you for a man ever again." His tone was even, but the red that flushed up his neck was an excellent indicator to the truth of his words.

I wanted to throw my hands in the air in defeat, but Mim was too important. I needed to find a way into the good graces of her father. "Are we finished here, sir? I have to take care of Judith. By the way, if you called the wing The Kent Center for Reproductive Health, I'm sure she'd write you a check tonight."

I found Mim with Judith looking over the model of the wing. It was a large undertaking and would require millions of dollars in backing.

"Hello, Luca. Mim was just telling me how you two met." Judith left Mim's side and rested her hand in the crook of my arm.

I placed my hand over hers and patted. "Did she also tell you she's ruined my social life by requiring me to present my graduate project three weeks early?"

"Good women always keep their men on their toes. Be a doll and guide me to that group in the corner." Judith pointed to a group in the corner that could rival England's queen for jewels. "It was nice meeting you, Mim."

"The pleasure was mine, Ms. Kent. See you soon, Luca."

Mim walked past me in the direction I had left her father. Would he tell her who I was? What I was? A smart man would, but something about Marcus Knight made me think he'd let Mim learn on her own, and the thought of her knowing sent a shiver clawing up my spine.

"Are you cold, Luca?"

"What? Cold? No." I rubbed her hand and led her to the group of women who welcomed Judith with open arms. After short introductions, I stepped back and leaned against the wall. I'd be close if Judith needed me, but in the meantime, I would scour the room for Mim.

After two full sweeps of the ballroom, I found her holding up the wall opposite me. She smiled and nodded as people walked past. Her eyes scanned the room until they settled on me, and my breath caught when her smile widened enough to reach her eyes.

She kicked off the wall and walked toward me, but I was working, and it wouldn't serve me well to get distracted, so I left my leaning post on the wall and sidled up to Judith.

"Can I get you ladies a drink?" I asked when a lull in the conversation presented itself.

Judith beamed at me as if my manners had made her proud. I took the women's drink orders and went off to fill their requests.

Five drinks was a tough balancing act, but I delivered each woman's cocktail—three dry martinis, a glass of chardonnay, and a scotch on the rocks for Judith. They were content once again.

Mim and I never crossed paths the rest of the night, and for that, I was both grateful and disappointed. By nine o'clock, my date was beginning to fade, so I placed her gently in her limousine to send her home.

The first thing she did was toe off her shoes, then she reached for the bottle of water tucked inside the drink holder.

After several sips, she said. "Luca, you were by far the most attentive and pleasant date I've had in a long time. I hear you're retiring soon. So much the pity, I could have enjoyed having you around again."

I leaned down and gave her a kiss on the cheek. "You are by far the best date I've had in a while as well."

Judith laughed. "Tell me that after your time with Marcus

Knight's daughter. Don't let him bully you. He's more like a rose petal than a thorn."

Judith slid across the black leather seat, and I closed the door. If all on-call dates were like this, I'd have signed up long ago.

Chapter 5

The morning began with a look at my new goal board. Once filled with pictures of material things, it now contained a graph. Lines in increments of a thousand dollars making their way up the page. With three regulars and Judith for two hours last night, I'd earned seventeen hundred and fifty dollars this week. I pulled the thick red sharpie from my backpack and filled the picture in up to that amount. Hitting sixty thousand was going to be tough, but this visual would remind me how far I needed to go so I wouldn't lose focus.

I checked my calendar to see if Sandra had filled in my weekend. I had a regular client on Friday night, but the rest of my time was free. My Saturday was marked off for two hours with Diane Westgate. I began to groan out loud, but I heard River's voice tell me if I made her feel beautiful, maybe she would become beautiful. At this point, I'd be happy if she resembled a woman.

Dressed in jeans and a long-sleeved Henley, I pushed myself through the crowded train to exit. With my project due early, I'd be spending a lot of time at the library if I wanted to finish on time.

Nut-brown carpet silenced the journey to my favorite corner table. Nestled behind the old classics, I inhaled the musty scent of aged paper and dust. The screen flickered as my computer sputtered to life. I'd need at least five years of stock exchange history for my study. What made one company successful and another fail?

My thoughts went straight to Sandra. She had a successful business model. The thing that made it work was she was always offering something new. Every year, shiny new pennies in the form of financially needy students were offered to her clients. Did they enjoy the unveiling as much as the service? Commodities came in every shape and form.

A laugh escaped me when I considered how easy it would be to write my project on the buying and selling of bodies. The trading of sex for dollars. Too bad it wasn't an option.

My afternoon filled with entry points and exit points, trade margins, indexes, and spreads. By one o'clock, my mind was foggy and my eyes blurred. I packed up my belongings and went in search of a double shot latte. I'd need it to keep my eyes open tonight.

When I entered the campus coffee shop, I found Mim in the corner. She was oblivious to my arrival. Her knees pulled to her chest, and a worn copy of *The Scarlet Letter* was in her hands.

I slid into the booth across from her with a honeyed chai tea offering. She turned to me, and her eyes rose from the book. "Our date isn't until seven."

"You're right. I'm just getting a jolt of caffeine so I can be alert when we're out." Compared to her chai, my coffee looked like mud.

"Are you insinuating that I'll be a bore and put you to sleep?" She closed her book and rotated her body.

Steam rose from the cup I'd pushed in front of her. "No, I'm just saying I'm tired, and I needed a little pick me up." I looked down at the book on the table. "*The Scarlet Letter?*"

"Have you ever read it? It's fascinating." She opened the book and read, *'Ah, but let her cover the mark as she will, the pang of it will be always in her heart.'* "Nathaniel Hawthorne understood guilt and sin."

The silt that was my coffee went down like poison. "It was required reading in high school."

"Could you imagine having to wear a red A on your chest because you had a child out of wedlock? What if you were forced to wear one for every premarital experience you'd had? Would your chest be full, Luca?" She tilted her head and waited for my response.

Liquid spurted from my mouth and nose. We grabbed napkins and cleaned up my mess while I tried to cough up the fluid that settled in my lungs. "I refuse to answer on the grounds it may incriminate me."

If I told the truth, there would be too many As to fit. I could embroider my entire wardrobe front and back, and it wouldn't come close to marking the times I'd sinned according to Nathaniel Hawthorne's ideals.

"Imagine Hester Prynne alive today. She'd be strutting around this campus with Pearl in tow, and no one would give her a second glance. Society judges too harshly."

Would Mim feel the same if she knew what I did for a living? Would she cross the street and walk away when I appeared, or would she embrace me? Hopefully, I'd never have to find out.

"You left early last night."

Mim blew on her tea. "Everyone interesting was already taken." A sexy smile curved her lips. She was flirting. "How was your evening with Judith? It appears The Kent Center for Reproductive Health is a reality, and my father says to thank you. Care to elaborate?" She slid her tongue across the lip of the cup, catching the dribble of honey left behind.

My whole body shuddered at the sight. Now I'd have to stay in the booth until the rise in my pants subsided. I felt like a teenage boy who had just seen his first naked boob.

"I have no idea. I got the impression your father didn't like me."

"He doesn't like anyone who's interested in me. Imagine living with a father who sees vaginas every day of the week. You could say my family is progressive when it comes to sex education, and now I'm pretty sure he regrets being so open."

"How many As would Ms. Knight have to plaster to her

chest if she were Hester?" It was a fair question. She'd asked the same of me, and I gave her an honest answer. The number of women would incriminate me.

"Not as many as you might think, but the day is still young." She gathered her things and shoved them into her leather backpack. "I have to rush home. I have a hot date tonight with an Italian guy." She slid out of the booth and stood in front of me.

"Don't get your hopes up; I'm an innocent Catholic boy." Those damn yoga pants left nothing to the imagination. I'd have to sit here another ten minutes before I could leave without embarrassing myself. How was I supposed to get through dinner?

"Something tells me you're not the person you show the world, Luca Gregorio, but I'm up for the challenge of peeling back your layers and seeing who you hide beneath that cocky skin of yours." She spun to her left and walked out the door.

There was no way she was peeling back anything. I'd have dinner with her, and that would be all. As much as I wanted more, I couldn't let Mim into my world. Her father was right, she deserved better. I wouldn't defile her with my filthy lifestyle.

Mim still had that light in her eyes that some called hope. Mine had dimmed temporarily, but I felt the spark ignite each time I was with her. I loved that she knew what she wanted and appeared to go after it. She was honest and forthright, whereas I was deceptive and evasive. She was everything virtuous and pure, and I was Hester Prynne with a penis.

An hour later, I was pacing my apartment. Would she come back here? Did I want her to? I'd never been so twisted by a woman in all my days. Everything in my head said cut and run, but my heart said something different.

Damn it.

I pulled my graph from the wall and tucked it into my closet. In the off chance she would visit, I didn't want to explain what the hell I was tracking.

A glance around my place revealed the ugly truth. I was in no position for company. When was the last time I'd made my bed? I'd washed my sheets weekly, but the last time I'd pulled the duvet up and over the pillows, I couldn't remember. Each room was studied with scrutiny. The pile of clothes in the corner was not attractive. The ties wrapped around my bedposts made it look like I had a bondage fetish. My bathroom was a disaster. The living room wasn't much better, and the kitchen should be condemned. I was stuck in a rut and living in a pigsty.

I'd spent too much time buried in guilt and debt. As I looked around my apartment—filth. This wasn't who I was. It was time to clean up my act.

I blew through my apartment with the force of a category five storm. In short order, I had the place looking neat and tidy. I'd never get the GQ award for bachelor pads or the Good Housekeeping seal of approval, but even Mom would have been proud of how clean it looked, and she was a tough sell on everything.

Like a teenage girl on her first date, I second-guessed every outfit I'd tried on. The suit was too formal. The tattered jeans too casual. When I walked out the door, I was dressed in khakis, a button-down shirt, and a tweed sports coat. For whatever reason, I always felt better covered up.

The cab pulled in front of her place with ten minutes to spare. My mother's mantra rang in my ear, *never be late for dinner or love.* I still didn't know what in the hell that meant, but it seemed like good advice.

When I rang the bell of the brownstone, I didn't expect Mr. Knight to answer the door. Apparently, Mim lived with her parents.

"Luca." His deadpan tone said it all.

"Mr. Knight, it's a pleasure to see you again."

I offered my hand, but he turned around and mumbled something as he walked away. I couldn't hear all the words, but *stubborn little asshole* was hard to miss.

At the bottom of the stairs, he yelled, "Miriam, that boy is here to see you." He gave me one last glance, then walked down the hallway.

Mim appeared like an angel at the top of the stairs. She floated down the steps in a soft pink dress and matching ballet flats. I loved that she was practical. Heels looked incredible on a woman, but wearing them for extended periods of time had to be painful.

"Sorry about my dad. He doesn't like you. He won't give me a reason; just says I could do better." When she reached the bottom step, she was only inches shorter than me. "I like you, so I'll have to hope that you grow on him." She lifted up onto her toes and pressed a soft kiss to my cheek.

The heat from her lips coursed through my body and wrapped around my heart. I knew right then I'd never cut and run. Mim didn't know me, she didn't have expectations, but she saw something in me I couldn't see in myself.

I placed her hand in mine and led her to the front door. "He's right. You could do better."

"Yeah, probably, but let's see where this goes." The setting sun left an orange glow as the day welcomed the night. She nudged me in the side. "Geno's is just a few blocks away. Have you ever been?"

I felt like a teenage boy on his first date. My fingers locked with hers, and my palm began to sweat. Our arms swung between us. If we were younger, I could see us skipping down the block together.

One right turn, one left turn, and a block ahead was Geno's. "Reservations for Knight at seven," Mim announced when we arrived at the hostess stand.

The hostess glanced at both of us, grabbed two menus, and guided us to a booth in the corner. She rattled off the daily specials, but I heard nothing. Mim enchanted me. She had pulled her hair to one side and twisted it, laying it on her shoulder. All I could think about was my lips on her neck.

She tapped my foot under the table. "Are you paying attention?"

"You distract me."

Her face lit up in spite of her feigned exasperation. "I was saying, they have the best bruschetta, but then the calamari is amazing, too." Her eyes sparkled like precious jewels in the light of the flickering candle between us. "What are you smiling at?" She glanced around, looking for the object of my delight.

"You. You make me happy. You're frustrating as hell, but your eyes captivate me, and your smile melts my heart."

She flicked her napkin open and placed it across her lap. "Is this where you pick up my hand and kiss my knuckles again? Smooth, Romeo, real smooth."

I knew she was joking. She'd been teasing me since the first day I'd kissed her hand, and yet here she was, having dinner with me. "Is this where you carve out my heart and ask the cook to sauté it in olive oil and garlic? Why are you so opposed to romantic gestures?"

"I'm not. I just don't know you well enough to recognize when you're sincere. You look like a playboy, but there is a glimpse of an altar boy that shows up when I least expect it." She drew lazy circles on the white tablecloth. "I watched you with Judith. You were the perfect gentleman. You doted on her and her friends. You laughed and joked with them. Every woman in that group felt like you were their date last night. Every one of those women would have paid to have you last night."

The sliding of my heart to my stomach caused acid to seep into my throat. Did Mim know? "I was just doing my job."

"Your job was to help out a friend, but you did more; you made an old woman feel young again. It showed in her smile when you kissed her cheek and closed the door to her car. Honestly, I was a bit jealous."

"You were jealous of Judith?" I couldn't imagine Mim being jealous of anyone.

"Yes, she got the kiss I wanted."

I slid closer, our thighs touched, and my heart began to race. "I hope you want a better kiss than that. I have a special one saved up for you."

"Really?" She blushed pink from her neck to her bangs.

Deep and throaty, I answered, "Absolutely—"

"Welcome to Geno's, can I get you something to drink?" The waiter stood before us with pen in hand. Maybe his intrusion was a blessing in disguise. I had a feeling if I had leaned over and kissed her, I wouldn't have stopped.

We ordered the bruschetta and the calamari, along with a bottle of cabernet and two orders of spaghetti and meatballs.

The conversation was light and airy the rest of the evening. Mim was an only child. Her mother was English, and her father was a yank, or so she said. Her parents met at Oxford, and the rest was history.

Mim spoke with an English accent, but there was a bit of an east coast twang that slipped in on occasion. When she said words like 'park', they sounded like 'pahk', and 'car' sounded like 'cah'. I thought it was charming until she punched me in the arm and told me not to pick on her.

Mim wasn't ready to go home after dinner, so she asked to go to her neighborhood park, the private park that belonged to residents only. She slid her key into the iron gate, and we entered paradise. Ivy grew up the fence, giving complete privacy to those on the inside. The trees were halfway in bloom. Some flowered, some were green with the young leaves of spring. We walked to a bench in the center. A fountain gurgled in the distance. The wind picked up and whipped around us.

Mim shuddered. Without asking, I removed my jacket and placed it on her shoulders. The tweed swallowed her up. With our legs touching, I wrapped my arm around her shoulders and pulled her into my side. She fit the space perfectly.

"We talked about me at the restaurant, Luca. Now I want to know about you." She snuggled into my side and rested her head against my chest. "Why finance?"

"I didn't want to be an electrician." I told her about the family business and explained my need to be independent.

"I understand, my dad had his heart set on me being a doctor. My mother wanted me to be a model or an actress. Sadly, I was too short, and I'm not a rule follower or good with direction."

"You? Not a follower? I don't believe it." I looked around the park and wondered if a moment could be more perfect.

"You work, right?" She rotated and turned her eyes up to me.

"Yes, I work for a concierge service." It wasn't a lie. I did work for a concierge service, but I had no intention of going into details. I didn't want to lie to Mim; every lie I told would come back to haunt me later.

"So you sell tickets and take people on tours?" She'd

curled into my body to borrow my warmth, and I was happy to give it. I was hot—hot for her.

"Something like that. I do what people need me to do. It pays well. I'm working on getting my foot in the door of a financial firm. What about you?"

"I work at the school. I'm a TA for two professors, and I scored a position in the finance department. It's been a good job. Managing students' loans keeps me busy."

Mine keep me busy, too. "You still live with your parents?" It wasn't as odd as it seemed, but she was employed and could afford to be on her own.

"At twenty-seven, I should be living on my own, but I have a pretty good deal at home. The second floor is mine. It has everything from its own kitchen, to a master suite and living room. Zero rent is a bonus. Makes it easy to save for a permanent place."

"Wow, that does sound amazing."

I couldn't imagine having those benefits. Maybe that's where Mim got her confidence. She didn't have to stress about everyday life. Instead, she could focus on planning her future. That had to raise self-assurance.

"Do you want to see it? I'd love to have you over." Mim stood and took my hand.

"Maybe someday, but I don't think your father would be happy if he found me in your home." In fact, I was sure Marcus Knight would be anything but happy.

On the stoop of her brownstone, I kissed her. It was a soul-searching, heart-stopping kiss I'd never forget. When she melted into my arms and welcomed my tongue into her mouth, I was a changed man. I'd wet my wick hundreds of times in the last two years, but that kiss was the most intimate moment of my existence.

I walked toward the subway with a smile as wide as the Hudson River plastered to my face.

Chapter 6

Mim had mentioned the night before that she left for work at half past seven, so at twenty minutes past the hour, I was standing outside her door with a steaming hot Chai tea with honey in my hand.

She backed out of her door dressed in a blue wrap around dress and black boots. When she turned, I was leaning against the wrought iron rail that flanked her front steps.

"Good morning." I pushed off the rail and offered her the tea.

Her smile was sun-warm and bright. "You're going to spoil me. What are you doing here?" She wrapped her arm around mine, and we walked toward the subway station.

"I didn't have anything going on this morning, so I thought I'd escort you to school. I'm trying to up my Romeo skills." Saying it out loud made me feel like I was back in high school, ready to carry my girlfriend's books. *Girlfriend?* No way. *Mim was just a bright spot in an otherwise dull day.* "After class, I'm stopping by the library for a while to do research for my project." I tried to frown at the mention of my project, but the way she twisted her lips and rolled her eyes made me laugh.

"Are you going to whine until May?"

"Maybe. Will it work in my favor?"

"Only if you want the pointy toe of my boot planted on your bum." She looked down at her shoes and faked a side-kick to my backside.

"I was hoping for something a bit more friendly."

I slid my arm up her back and wrapped it around her shoulder. In her heels, she was still a head shorter than me. Her small stature was misleading because she carried herself like a linebacker intent on winning the Super Bowl. She was formidable, a perfect mixture of sweetness and strength.

"I'll show you friendly." She stopped at the corner and pulled me down by the collar of my oxford shirt. When we kissed, she bit down on my lower lip and nibbled. Holy hell, if that wasn't the hottest kiss ever.

"I like your version of friendly." I stilled and took her in. She wasn't what I needed at this time in my life, but I'd be damned if I could let her go. Those damn expressive eyes and full, kissable lips had jumbled my senses.

"I like you, too, Luca. Who knew you'd be the perfect escort, and I thought you were just a pretty face." She cupped my cheek and rubbed her fingers across my scruff.

No words were ever truer. I wasn't perfect, but I was

certainly an escort. However, when I was with her, I was just Luca Gregorio, and that suited me perfectly.

We exchanged numbers on the subway. When we reached the university, I walked her to the finance building. She wouldn't be in class today, so I gave her a kiss she'd remember and walked away.

At nine o'clock, my phone buzzed with a message from Mim.

Dinner tonight? My place at six?

Mim

Sadly, I wouldn't be able to get together with her tonight. I had a client to service. Talbot was easy, she had a fetish, but generally speaking, an hour was all she needed. It was a bummer that our appointment was at seven. Not enough time before dinner, and too late to eat after.

I'm working tonight and tomorrow night. Want to spend the day together tomorrow?

Luca

I held my cell phone waiting for her to reply. It took her ten minutes. I'd just about given up when her message came through.

Sorry, I have to work. Imagine that? I'm disappointed you're booked for the night. I was hoping to see you, but I suppose I'll have to wait until the morning. Be at my house at nine. I have time to take you to my favorite place for eggs.

And there was bossy Mim again. She didn't ask, she demanded, and I didn't mind. I liked that she knew what she wanted. It took the confusion out of things.

I'll be there.

Luca

After class, I spent hours in the library looking at a computer screen until it blurred. That's when I knew I'd looked at numbers long enough. The trek through campus led me to the commons area where I heard my name called from across the lawn.

I shaded my eyes with my hand and scoured the area. Standing in front of the coffee shop was Father Tobin. I'd spent nearly two years on this campus, and not once had I run into a priest. I held up my hand and waved, but he flagged me over. My stomach lurched, then tightened.

"Hey Father, how are you?"

The young priest opened the door of the coffee shop and ushered me inside. What was it these days with pushy people? First Mim, and now Father Tobin. It was obvious I was giving off a vibe that said I needed guidance, at least where the priest was concerned. He seemed to be showing up everywhere.

"I'm good, Luca. More importantly, how are you? You've been on my mind lately. Coffee or tea?"

"Nothing for me. Did you need something?" I looked around to see why he would summon me, but there were no massive vases of flowers or broken down pipe organs. The only people present were a few students. The smell of freshly ground coffee beans filled the air.

"No, I thought we could have a chat. I think you need something, Luca. I'm not sure what it is, but I see it in your eyes. Maybe I could help with that." He ordered two cups of coffee and handed one to me.

Obviously, I was having coffee with the priest. "Why are you on campus?" We walked to the end of the counter where the milk and sugar were kept. I poured enough milk into my coffee for it to become a latte. Tobin poured enough sugar into his cup to go into a diabetic coma.

"I teach a theology class on Fridays." He led me to the booth where I had sat with Mim. I slid to the side where she had been reading *The Scarlet Letter*.

"That makes sense. I'm not usually here this late on Fridays, but I was working on my research in the library." I was also fantasizing about Mim, but the priest would never understand. I studied Father Tobin for a long minute. His blond hair was cut military style, off the collar and above the ears. Many would consider him handsome. "How does one stay celibate?" I didn't realize my thought had been vocalized.

"Well, that's a question many ponder, but few have the courage to ask." Father Tobin folded his napkin in half and placed his cup on top of it.

"I'm sorry, I seemed to blurt out a thought. You don't have to answer." In all honesty, I was curious how a man could give up the very act that made him feel like a man.

"Everything we do requires choices. I dated in school. I had a girlfriend for quite a while, and I'm certainly not a virgin. But one day I woke up and had an unquenchable desire to serve God, that was stronger than my physical desire."

"I could never be a priest."

"You can be anything you want to be as long as you're honest with yourself. Are you honest with yourself, Luca?" Father Tobin pinned me with his eyes.

"I'm a realist, Father."

"Are you?" Father Tobin rubbed his finger and thumb over his chin. "When I look at you, I see a man in turmoil. A man trying to find a balance between who he is and who he wants to show the world."

"I'm in a transitional phase in my life. I'm figuring it out."

Was I trying to convince him or myself? I had roughly eleven weeks to live in my fake world, and then I'd be free to live authentically. I had a new take on things. Mim was the light at the end of a dark tunnel for me. I could get through the following weeks knowing I could eventually give myself over to her. "Listen, Father, I have to run. I have to hit the gym and get cleaned up before I go to work. It's been nice chatting."

"Come to the church on Sunday, Luca. Mass is every hour until noon." He slid out of the booth and patted my back. It was a kinder and gentler pat than he gave me the other day. This one felt like encouragement.

"I heard you accept saints and sinners."

"That we do because you know what? We all rotate between the two. We're human."

Strenuous workouts at the gym often cleared my head, but today my workout had me thinking about Mim.

"Get your head in the game." Jack pulled the weights I struggled with up to the bar. "What the hell is wrong with you lately?"

"I'm under a lot of stress."

"Then sweat it out."

Jack pulled twenty pounds off the bar but upped my reps. He wasn't going to let me slack off. He never did.

"I only have you for a couple of months, I'm leaving my job, and this perk will go with it." Leaving the athletic club would be good. Every time I came here was a reminder of my responsibility to stay fit, but hard bodies weren't the only hard requirement.

By the time I finished with Jack, I was drenched in sweat. He must have felt like it was his duty to give me my money's worth. I'd be feeling the burn for days.

Back at my building, Italian workers were laying travertine tile when I arrived. They looked up and snickered while they called me 'pretty boy' and made fun of my suit. Little did they know, I spoke fluent Italian, and when I told them this pretty boy made three hundred and fifty dollars an hour wearing this suit, they shut up and went back to grouting.

My apartment felt different. Gone was the weight of disappointment that hid in the dirty dishes and laundry, and in its place were hope and a glimpse of happiness. Even pulling my research from my backpack didn't seem overwhelming or depressing.

I had this. I could do it.

The next hour was spent creating graphs for my assignment. Visuals were always good. People tended to believe what they saw.

The familiar ding of my phone pulled me from my creative corner where I'd color-coded the gains and losses of the top one hundred companies traded on the NYSE for the last five years.

Have a good night. Don't work too hard.

This feeling of bliss at seeing Mim's simple message was new to me. Was this how real happiness felt? I didn't need hundred dollar bills shoved down my trousers to make me smile. I just needed a little powerhouse of a woman to wish me a happy day. Who knew life could be that simple?

I'd rather be with you.

Luca

She responded right away.

Call in sick and come over.

Having that option would have been nice, but I had my eye on the finish line.

That would be irresponsible and certainly wouldn't help with my student loans.

Luca

She wouldn't understand firsthand about student loans. Her father indisputably paid for her education. Mim lived a life of privilege. She lived in a fancy brownstone, went to fancy fundraisers, and wore couture clothes, and yet she always seemed grounded. She was a conundrum to me. She was bossy, yet soft. Haughty, yet humble. Simple, but also complex.

Can't blame a girl for trying. I'll see you tomorrow.

Tomorrow couldn't come fast enough for me, and it wouldn't get here until today was over, so I showered, dressed, and left for my next client.

Jessica lived on Fifth Avenue, not too far from where Jade and River lived. Her flat sat high on the fifty-sixth floor and overlooked the city.

Jessica was an unusual client. She was the Vice President for Global Finance, her father's company. They specialized in international trade. I don't know what molded her love life or lack thereof. She wasn't ugly, nor beautiful either, but she was sweet, and she had a weird fetish. She preferred a vibrator to a man, but the vibrator didn't give her the one thing a man could—hot semen on her body. I provided that.

The doorman smiled as I entered. He knew me by name. I'd been coming, literally, for almost two years.

"Hey, Luca." Sam pulled the door open for me.

"Can you tell her I'm on my way up?" I slipped him a ten and stepped in front of the elevator.

"You got it."

I walked into the waiting car and zipped up to the fifty-sixth floor. There were only two units per floor. Off to the right was Jessica's.

She opened the door when I arrived. "Hey, how are you? I ordered Chinese." She was dressed in jeans and a pink T-shirt. At thirty-six, she still looked like a teen. Her brown hair was pulled back in a high ponytail and bounced back and forth as she walked down the hallway.

"Did you get my favorite?" This was part of our routine.

We had dinner, chatted about TV and sports. Sometimes we played a game. I never knew if I'd be here for an hour or three. I just went with the flow.

Jessica was misunderstood. I imagine people never gave her the benefit of the doubt since she inherited her job, but she was smart and capable. Her privileges limited her life.

Was it the same for Mim?

Jessica never knew who to trust or what their motives were. I suppose that was why it worked for her and me. She knew what motivated me to show up every Friday like clockwork. I was like a scheduled manicure in a way.

"Yep, crispy duck for you, and Moo Goo Gai Pan for me." We sat at the black lacquered table and ate.

"How was work?" I always started our conversation out the same. She was comfortable with talking about work, and I always gained something from the details she shared.

"Good. We're expanding in Singapore. My dad wants me to take over that market, but I'm not sure I want to do that. I like it here." She glanced around her apartment. The simplicity of the modern architecture blended in with the city outside. Crisp, bold colors bounced off the abstract art that lined the walls. Everything else was black, white or red. This was her—bright, bold and honest.

"It could be good. You could get away from your dad and establish yourself without his influence. Maybe find a boyfriend..." I rarely brought up outside relationships, but having spent the last few days with Mim gave me a new perspective on how much happiness the right person could bring to my life.

She spooned a healthy serving of chicken and button mushrooms onto her plate. "Now you're dreaming. You think most guys would put up with me? I'm in love with batteries, silicone, and the low rumble of my rabbit's motor." She popped a mushroom into her mouth.

I opened the box of crispy duck and inhaled the thick, smoky scent. "Men have just as many fetishes as women. There is someone for everyone."

"What about you? Are you going to find a girlfriend— someone you can share more than your dick with?"

"I met someone recently that could be that girl. Right now, I refuse to share my dick with her, not that she's asked. This," I pointed to the crotch of my pants, "is simply a work tool right now."

That was the thing I liked about my time with Jessica. We didn't pretend it was a date. In fact, we had built a friendship on the honesty of what we were to each other. I was hot semen, and she was a regular deposit into my account. There was something beautiful about our lack of pretenses.

"Luca, that's great. Just don't screw it up."

"I'm doing my best not to. I'm walking a slippery slope right now. She doesn't know I do this for a living."

"I don't think I'd tell her."

"Good advice."

We chatted about funny things, like why hot dogs come in packages of ten and buns come in packages of eight. Why airline travel is supposed to be safe, but they call the airport a terminal. Our final thought before we headed to her bed was why they don't make cat-flavored dog food.

She opened her drawer and looked over her collection of rabbit vibrators. She chose the pink one that matched her T-shirt. I stood at the end of the bed and tugged her jeans off. She never wore underwear. I didn't know if it was something she only omitted on our Friday nights or something she practiced with regularity.

I pointed to her cotton tee. "Your shirt, off or on?" I slouched out of my sports coat and pulled my shirt over my head. She liked me bare-chested.

"Off today. I want to feel you come on my breasts." She tugged her pink cotton tee off and released her bra clasp to let her girls fly.

It was funny how I could see Mim in a sexual way, but when I looked at Jessica, I might as well have been a construction worker and her body a hammer. All in a day's work.

She lubed up her device and went to work. She had it down to an art, and lately, it was a game to see if I could jerk myself to climax as she reached hers. I unzipped my pants and gripped myself. Thumb on top and three fingers placed in the perfect position with the perfect amount of pressure, I stood between her legs and began to stroke myself.

I knew she was getting close by the way she tensed her thighs and her back rose from the mattress. "Wait for me, Jessica." I gripped harder and tugged faster.

"Damn it, Luca, I'm cresting." Her moans became loud while her body quaked.

I closed my eyes and pictured Mim. In my imagination, she was the one holding my hardness and every stroke was her doing. My body exploded hot strings over Jessica's breasts. While I fantasized about Mim, Jessica writhed against a silicone penis that would emasculate most men.

Like usual, I lay down beside her while she caught her breath. Her hands slid over the slickness on her chest. She loved the feel, the salty taste, and the texture. Who was I to argue? She paid me a lot of money for a teaspoon of ejaculate.

"Thanks, Luca. I know this would be weird for most, but you've always given me what I needed without question." She wiped her chest off with her T-shirt. When she turned on her side, I pulled her into my arms.

"We all have our things." The truth was, I was a vanilla guy on my own. I'd experienced enough kink to last a lifetime. I didn't need whips, toys, or bondage to get me off. All I wanted was to feel love when I made love.

Chapter 7

I t was just shy of nine o'clock when I called Mim. "What are you doing?" I asked when she answered on the first ring.

"Grading papers for Saunders. Are you on a break?" There was a crinkling noise in the background.

I leaned against the black iron railing of her front steps. "I'm off for the night, and I'm on your porch." I'd stepped on the subway with every intention of going home, but I'd found myself on the line that led to her place. "I thought about getting ice cream. Would you care to join me?"

"Is that even a question? Anything to save me from grading papers. I'll be right down."

When the door flew open, she ran into my arms. "And I thought I was just a distraction from grading papers." I ran my fingers through her hair and pulled her to me. When I pressed my lips against hers, all thoughts of Rocky Road left my mind. I could be satisfied standing here consuming the sweetness of her mouth.

Her hands roamed my chest. She pushed her body into mine, forcing my hardening length to press against her hip. If we didn't get moving, I'd break the rule I had about public sex and take her right here on the front stoop.

It took every bit of strength to break away. Everything about her drew me in. She was the yin to my yang. The light to my darkness. She smelled like lilacs and tasted like honey. I felt like a hungry bee around her.

I entered ice cream into my phone, and we followed the directions to Dixon's. It was two doors down from Geno's. Mim ordered a banana split, while I went with my old standby of Rocky Road.

She ate her banana split one flavor at a time, starting with the chocolate. "I'm glad you got off early."

Sometimes her wording held double meaning for me. How close she came to the truth scared me. "I only had one thing to take care of, and it was quick and easy. I bet you haven't spent many Friday nights alone."

"If you want to know about my past dating life, ask. I'm an open book, Luca. I value honesty above all else." She moved on to the vanilla scoop.

I was screwed. I could love her. I could respect her, and I could give her everything but complete honesty. "When was your last relationship, and why did it end?"

"It was with a guy named Mike, and it ended because he couldn't handle the strength of my personality. We broke up about six months ago. I decided against dating until I found someone special. That guy was you."

"I like your strength, but I'm Italian, and most Italian women are ball busters, so you feel like home to me." Of course, that called for a kiss, and in the process, I dumped my cone on the ground.

"Let's go back to my place. We can watch a movie or talk." She didn't wait for my response; she turned toward her house and marched up the street with purpose.

I'd follow her anywhere, but her house was the least appealing place for me to be. One floor down, her father would be judging me.

When we entered the brownstone, I eyed the main level looking for her dad until she led me upstairs into her apartment. Decorated in warm, earthy tones, it was inviting and comfortable. With a living room, a kitchen, and a small dining area, it was spacious. I assumed there would be a bedroom and a bathroom down the narrow hallway, but I didn't ask, and she didn't offer to show it to me. When she went to the kitchen to make tea, I walked around her place and looked at the pictures that lined her bookshelves. There were photos of her in front of a pyramid, the Eiffel Tower, Big Ben, and the Taj Mahal. She'd been all over the world. She lived a life most people would dream about. She could have her pick of anyone, and yet here I was in her apartment, getting ready to watch a movie and drink tea.

Why me?

I picked up a picture of Mim standing in front of a cherry blossom tree. Her father smiled in the photo, but his eyes appeared to bore into me. I put the picture down and walked away. When I turned around, his knowing blue eyes seemed to follow me. No matter where I stood, he stared.

"What are you doing?" Mim walked toward me with a tray containing a teapot, two cups, honey, and cream.

I looked back at the photo. "I'm trying to find a place where I can stand and your dad isn't staring at me with a look that says *get out of my daughter's house.*" I took the tray from her hands and set it on the coffee table in front of us.

"I know, weird, right? The light hit his eyes in just a way that they seem to follow you around." She walked to the shelf and lowered the picture face down. "You don't have to worry about my dad. Once he gets to know you, he'll like and respect you."

Fat chance of that. The man knew who I was, and he'd already warned me off his daughter once. The problem was, I couldn't stay away from her. I felt something for Mim I hadn't felt for anyone in years. I'd boxed up and buried my emotions long ago, but Mim with her quick wit and sass tore into my once impenetrable shield.

"What are we watching?" I asked.

Mim poured tea and doctored it with honey and milk before she slid next to me on the couch. She curled her legs up and leaned into my body. It felt natural to put my arm around her and pull her close.

"Comedy, drama, thriller, or love story?" She pulled up the on-demand menu and waited for my answer.

"I love scary movies, but I'll watch anything with you." I

sipped the tea she'd prepared. It was the perfect mix of creamy and sweet.

"Scary it is, then." She scrolled through the menu and chose the movie *Sinister*. "Have you seen this movie?" She pressed play and snuggled in closer.

Somewhere deep inside, I hoped she scared easily. I'd be happy to have her jump in my lap during an intense scene.

It didn't take long for the movie to turn dark. When Ellison found the Super 8 videos in the attic, I knew I'd get my wish. By the fifteen-minute mark, Mim was sitting in my lap with a blanket pulled up to her nose, her eyes peeking above it.

Mim was a powerhouse, but deep inside she was just as vulnerable as the rest of us. Privilege didn't make her stronger or braver. It just gave her different options.

When the credits rolled, I turned her on my lap and ran the backside of my fingers down her cheek. She was smooth and perfect. She reminded me of an airbrushed picture, without a blemish or freckle to mar her skin.

"You're so beautiful. Why me, Mim?"

Her eyes held a thousand messages, all of them filled with kindness. She touched her lips to mine and spoke. "You had the courage to call me on my shit that first day. I like a man who isn't afraid to be honest about who he is, and what he feels."

She captured my mouth with hers and deepened the kiss. By the time I broke free, she was breathless and squirming in my lap. The motion of her bottom moving against my dick only increased the tension that grew in my jeans. Her words increased the tension that grew in my heart. I'd never lied to her, but I'd skated the truth several times. I wasn't ready to confess my sins to anyone at this point, and I knew if I stayed any longer, I'd want to be skin to skin with this woman. To move forward, I'd have to go back and tell her everything from the beginning.

Not gonna' happen; tonight was too perfect to ruin.

"I gotta go." I slipped out from under her and grabbed my jacket from the back of the couch.

"Don't go." She rose from the sofa and wrapped her hands around my waist.

"I have to go, Mim. You're too tempting, and I don't want what's happening between us to be a temporary thing. I want more." I couldn't believe I'd confessed my inner feelings to her. I wasn't even aware of them myself until the words spilled from my mouth. "I'll be here at nine."

After another heart-stilting kiss at her door, I raced down the steps and out the front entrance, where I came to a dead stop after I bounced off her father. He was looking none too happy to see me.

"Mr. Knight." I nodded my head at him.

"Luca, you have perfect timing. Stay there a moment." He unlocked the front door for Mrs. Knight and saw her safely inside.

Mim got her good looks from her mother. She was a stunning woman—petite and feminine, with the same dark chocolate hair as Mim. The only difference was in the eyes; whereas her mother had emerald green eyes, Mim's were as blue as the Caribbean Sea.

I was leaning against the wrought iron rail when Marcus Knight appeared.

"Let's walk, Luca." Marcus looked over his shoulder toward the door. I wondered what Mim would do if she knew her father was going to give me a tongue-lashing. "You're in need of money, and I can help. What will it take to get rid of you?"

His words stung. This wasn't how I'd envisioned my relationship with my girlfriend's father. *Girlfriend?* My heart had made the decision before my mind could catch up.

"I know how you feel about me, but I'm not the man you assume I am."

"Do you have sex for money, Luca?" The impact of each word felt like a dagger to my soul.

"Yes." How could I deny the truth? I pleasured women for a living, but it wasn't who I was.

"Are you having sex with my daughter?"

"No. I refuse to have sex with her until I've left the service." Did I see relief in his expression? "I care about your daughter. She's an amazing woman."

"Yes, she is, and I want her to stay that way. I appreciate your honesty, Luca. I don't know your story or what brought you to the point where you had to make the decisions you did, but you're not right for Mim."

"Don't judge me on my past, let me prove my worth to you. I'm a good man, and I won't hurt Mim." I prayed I could keep that promise. I never wanted to hurt her. I wanted to make her happy, to be the reason behind her brilliant smile.

We had walked a block before he stopped. "You'll hurt her

by not being honest with her. You'll hurt the both of you." He buttoned up his jacket as the wind whipped around the corner. "I love my daughter, and I don't want to see her hurt. Make the right decisions, Luca. Show me you're a good man. I have a feeling you are. Prove me right."

I jammed my hands into my jeans pockets. "Are you asking me to step away? If you are, I can't do it. Mim makes me want to be a better man. I promise I'll do right by her."

"I'll be keeping my eyes open, Luca." He turned and started to walk away, but he stopped and said, "Get tested before you ever sleep with my daughter. You owe her that much."

What Marcus didn't know was I got tested every month. I practiced safe sex, but things, like Claire dropping to her knees and sucking my dick, happened on occasion.

When I reached my apartment, I felt defeated. How could I have a relationship with Mim when her father was dead set against it? *Prove him wrong.* The words echoed in my brain. I deserved good things, too, and I would prove myself worthy.

I tossed and turned the entire night. One question invaded my thoughts. Should I come clean with Mim before things became more serious? Was not telling her everything, lying? I decided if she asked for specifics, I'd give them to her. Otherwise, I'd keep those details to myself.

Chapter 8

At exactly nine o'clock, I stood on Mim's porch with her favorite tea in my hand. I called her number and waited for her to answer.

"Hello, sexy. I'll be right down." She didn't give me a chance to respond before she hung up, but she was out the front door within seconds.

Dressed in jeans and a purple cotton tee, she looked like a teenager. Her long hair was pulled back into a clip, and her face was free of makeup.

Many women needed the addition of makeup to enhance their looks, but Mim could never be described as plain. She had thick, dark eyelashes that fluttered against her cheeks when she closed her eyes. She flushed with a rosy glow, and her lips were a natural raspberry red, so succulent that I craved to feast on them all day.

"Good morning, beautiful." I handed her the tea and

snuck in a quick kiss before we walked down the steps. "You look pretty spry for nine o'clock on a Sunday."

She shook her head. "My parents like seven o'clock Mass." Her fingers traced the dark circles under my eyes. "What kept you up? You look tired." She dropped her hand and laced her fingers with mine.

"I've got a lot on my mind, but mostly I was thinking about you, and how quickly I'm falling for you."

Shit. What the hell was wrong with me? I had dysentery of the mouth. When I was with her, all of my real feelings seemed to find their way from my heart to my lips without stopping to check with my brain first.

She squeezed my hand. "I like that you're falling for me. It's such a shit show when you're alone in an emotion like that." She leaned her head on my arm, and we walked the four blocks to her favorite egg place, The Yellow Vase.

We sat at the counter in front of the window and watched people pass by as she ate her corned beef hash and eggs and I devoured a western omelet.

"'Mim' is an unusual name. I heard your dad call you Miriam at the fundraiser. Is that your real name?" The city was bustling with life. Even on Sunday, nothing slowed down.

"Miriam is my grandmother on my mum's side. It was too grown up of a name when I was little, so my parents called me Mim, and it stuck." She sipped at the fresh tea she ordered. "Miriam is way too regal for me. I'm more Mim than Miriam. Maybe someday I'll grow into it." She shrugged her shoulders.

"I like Mim; it's unique like you. I also love the way you say 'mum'. It's so sweet, but how in the heck did you manage to mix an English accent with the Jersey Shore?" I knew she'd want to reach out and slug me, and she did, right in the muscle of my right arm. "Ouch."

"Jersey Shore? I do not sound like I'm from Jersey. I'm a hybrid New Yorker, with a lot of East Coast influence. I probably picked up a bit more than I should have from one of the nuns at my school, but I loved her, and I copied her speech patterns and mannerisms. If you don't like my diction, you'll have to speak to Sister Roberta West."

"Catholic school?"

"Yes. You?"

I placed two twenties on the table and walked Mim out of the restaurant. "I don't think there's a Gregorio around who hasn't been Catholic school educated. My parents would have it no other way. There are five of us boys, and I'm sure Saint Mary's will be happy when the last of us graduates next year."

"Are all of your brothers as cute as you?"

"Are you looking for a new Italian boyfriend?" We walked hand in hand down the street. "I have four brothers who would fall helplessly in love with you in an instant, but then I'd have to kill them. I'm not great at sharing."

"I'm not good at sharing either." She ran her hand up my arm and hugged it tightly. "Are you my boyfriend, Luca?"

"I'd like to be." Her father wouldn't be happy, but knowing she was mine would help get me through the next couple months, and during that time I would make her feel like the most cherished and loved of all girlfriends.

"I'd like that, too. Now take me to your apartment. I want to see where my boyfriend lives."

"It's going to be a disappointment compared to your place." What would she think when she saw my little apartment? "I'll take you there, but you can't judge me, okay? I'm a poor college student." At least it was clean.

We jumped on the subway and exited about twenty minutes later. I lived near Soho, which was a pretty hip place to live, but my apartment was blocks away from the best neighborhood. All in all, it was safe, convenient, and affordable by New York standards.

"Posh tile in the entry." She looked at the travertine tile that had been recently installed. My landlord was doing some upgrades, and I hoped it wouldn't raise my rent.

Posh? Her English side was showing itself again. "Yes, it's new, but I liked the old tile. It felt like home, but I'm getting used to this tile. It's pretty swanky."

"Swanky? Who says that?"

"My dad."

"I'd love to meet your parents someday." She followed me up three flights of stairs. "It's no wonder your legs are as solid as steel." She used the handrail to drag herself up the last few steps.

"You noticed." She'd been checking out my legs at the gym. "Between the stairs and the gym, I stay in decent shape."

I slid my key into the lock and opened the door. I breathed deeply when we entered, praying my apartment didn't smell like sweaty socks or some other kind of funk, but all I smelled was my cologne.

"It smells like you." She walked into my home, and it immediately felt warm and cozy. "Your cologne has a hint of cinnamon that I love." She pulled me down and buried her nose into the curve of my neck. "It's Burberry, isn't it?"

"You have a good nose." I walked her deeper into my apartment and closed the door. "Can I get you something? I have regular tea, not Tetley or PG Tips, but I'll get some for the future, along with honey and milk. Otherwise, I have diet soda, coffee, and water."

"Nope, I don't need anything. Just a tour."

Without waiting for me, she wandered down the short hallway to my bedroom. It wasn't anything fancy. It had a queen-sized bed and dresser. My clothes had been picked up from the corners, and my ties had been removed from the bed frame. It looked tidy, although a bit plain.

She sat on the edge of my bed and bounced. Against my better judgment, I leaped on the mattress with her and pulled her into my arms. We were a mess of limbs and lips. I slipped my hand under her T-shirt and cupped her breast. Her nipple hardened and puckered against her lacy bra. I ran my thumb across the crest and soaked in the tiny moan that came from her mouth. I crushed my lips against hers and explored every dip and crevice. Our tongues danced to a heated beat.

She ran her hands under my shirt and let her fingertips graze over the muscles that were now clenched across my stomach. Up and down she scaled my chest and stomach until her hand rested on the rise in my pants. I growled when she firmly stroked me. God, she was making this hard.

I pulled her hand away and brought her fingertips to my lips. I kissed one finger at a time while I spoke. "We. Are. Not. Doing. This. Now." On the last word, I pressed a kiss to her palm.

"Why not?"

"Because you deserve to be wined and dined before I make love to you. I want you to be in love with me before you love me."

She turned her head like a confused puppy. "It's sweet that you're so old-fashioned, but I'm a modern woman, and I can handle sex before love."

I lay on my side and looked into her expressive eyes. "I get that you're a modern woman. It's one of the things I admire about you." I caressed her cheek with my thumb. "When we make love, I want it to be special. Commonplace sex happens all the time, but you deserve more than that."

She exhaled with what sounded like disappointment. "Luca, I imagine sex with you is anything but commonplace." We stayed on my bed and held each other for a few more minutes.

"What do you want to do?" I asked. She looked at me with an expression that said, *duh.* "Besides that?"

"Do you have a deck of cards?"

Once she skunked me in poker several times, we snuggled on my couch and watched mindless TV. Somewhere between reruns of The Big Bang Theory and whatever she was watching now, I'd fallen asleep. My head was cradled in her lap, and her fingers slid through my hair.

I stayed and pretended I was asleep while her fingers massaged my scalp. Tingles skittered through my body. I never wanted to move. When her stomach grumbled, I stirred.

"Hey, you had a good nap. Do you feel more rested?" She looked down at me, and sunshine escaped from her smile.

"I'm sorry. I'm so tired. Yes, I feel great, but you are obviously hungry. Let's get you fed." I reluctantly left the pillow of her thighs and stood. My back popped as I stretched my arms to the sky. "How about the corner deli?"

"Do they make a decent Rueben?" She ran her hand down her shirt and jeans, pressing away the wrinkles I had created.

"It's New York; you can't get a bad Reuben." I picked up my jacket and helped her into hers.

"I'm buying," she said while we trudged down the three flights of stairs. "I can't have you paying for everything."

"Nope, it's not the way I was raised, or the way I roll."

I couldn't afford to take her out to eat all the time. My new circumstances made it prohibitive, but there was no way she was paying for anything. I'd figure it out. Maybe Diane would be a good tipper. An audible groan at the thought of seeing Diane tonight escaped from my lips.

"Why the groan?" She didn't miss a thing, and I wondered how long it would take before she began to ask the difficult questions.

"Just thinking about having to work when I'd rather be watching scary movies with you."

"You could call in sick." She gave me a sneaky little smile just before she walked into Jerry's Deli.

"You are always telling me to call in sick. How many times have you called in sick?"

"Never."

"Me either. I was raised with a strong work ethic. My father wouldn't put up with us being irresponsible." He didn't put up with much, which was why it was so important to break out of the mold he had created for me.

"What do you have to do tonight?" We stood in line and waited for our turn to order.

The question threw me. I wasn't sure what I'd have to do tonight. All I knew was that a car was coming for me at seven. The rest was up to Diane.

"I don't know exactly, I suppose I'll find out when I get there. It's something different every time."

That answer seemed to satisfy her question. When we made it to the front of the line, we both ordered Reubens, and Mim pulled out her card before I could pull out my cash. I wasn't happy about her paying, but I showed her my gratitude with a kiss.

We brought our sandwiches, drinks, and chips to the park across the way and sat on the grass to eat.

"What are your plans after graduation?" She bit into her sandwich, and a bit of dressing ran out of the corner of her lip. I swiped it off and licked my finger before she could get her napkin to her lips. "Hey, eat yours. That was mine," she teased.

"I'm going to find a job. That's what I'm working on right

now. Some of the clients at the service I work for have connections to the finance world. I'm trying to see if I can get a foot in the door through those connections." It felt good to be talking about the future, and everything I said was spot on. No lies there.

"I'd be extra nice to those people. You never know where they can lead you."

If only she knew how nice I could be. Someday soon, I'd get to show her. She'd be lying beneath my body while I showered her with my brand of niceness.

"Enough about work. What's your plan for the rest of the weekend?"

Her lips puckered into a frown. "I'm grading papers the rest of the weekend. My *boyfriend* distracted me, and now I'm behind schedule."

"What an awful guy. Well, my *girlfriend* cut my project deadline by three weeks."

"What an awful girl." She rolled her eyes in that cute way she did the day I met her. "I bet she would be willing to help you."

"She would, but that would lead to other distractions, so I suppose I'll have to live without her for the rest of the weekend."

A day without Mim was going to be miserable, but I needed to work on my project, and she would be a distraction. I'd never get past her lips and into my project if we were together.

We finished up our lunches and walked to the subway

station. I was intent on taking her home, but she insisted on going by herself.

"Luca, I'm a grown woman who knows how to use the subway. Besides, you have to work on your project before you go to work."

'Work' was a dirty word right now. Work meant Diane, and I wasn't ready for her.

"Mim, what makes you feel beautiful?" How was I supposed to make Diane feel beautiful when she looked like a truck had hit her?

"You make me feel beautiful."

"No, I mean what exactly makes you feel beautiful?"

She leaned against the subway tiles, her expression contemplative. "The unexpected simple things make me feel beautiful. When you brought me tea with the perfect amount of honey and milk, that made me feel beautiful because you were paying attention. It showed that you valued more than my looks. When you listed off the drinks you had at your house and said you'd get English tea for me, that showed you knew what I liked. To be seen makes a woman feel beautiful." She slid into my body and tilted her head up to me. "I'm a goddess when I'm with you."

"You are the most amazing woman, Mim Knight, and I will make you happy." I took her lips in a slow, sensual kiss that left us both wanting more.

"You already make me happy. I'll see you Monday in class."

She skipped down the stairs and into the station, and I walked home with a full heart.

Chapter 9

At seven o'clock, I was downstairs, climbing into a black town car. Diane was dressed in a black suit very similar to my blue one. I slid in next to her and placed a simple kiss on her cheek.

"Hi, Diane."

I turned in my seat so I could look at her. Really look at her. If I were going to get through the next few months with her as my Saturday regular, I would need to find something about her that was pleasant.

"Luca, it's good to see you again."

Was her voice always so sweet and feminine? I don't remember her having any girly qualities. "What did you have in mind for tonight?"

She sat upright and faced forward. "I'd like to pretend we're on our first date. I've never really been on a date." She turned her head and smiled, but her smile couldn't mask the apprehension I saw flash across her brown eyes.

"Okay." I knocked on the window and told the driver to take us to Maxi's. It was a little French café off the beaten path. "I hope you like French because where I'm taking you has the best Coq au Vin around, and wait until you taste the crème brûlée."

A smile spread across her face. Her lips were thin, but her teeth were perfectly straight and white. I found myself wanting to make her smile. I wasn't interested in having sex with her, but I was intrigued by the challenge River had put before me. I would find the beauty in this woman.

We arrived at the restaurant and were seated immediately. I ordered the wine first, and while we waited for our Coq au Vin, we got to know each other. Our first meeting was entirely different, and I didn't know if it was because I was no longer in a position to choose, or if I'd matured in the time that had passed.

"Do you like your job, Diane?" I looked at her like she was all that existed. To be seen was what Mim said made her feel beautiful.

"The job, yes. The people, no."

"Tell me about them."

"There's not much to tell. I've been one of the guys my whole life, but at the office, I don't fit in." She sipped her wine. The silence settled around us.

"What do mean you've been one of the guys all your life?" What made her want to be one of the guys? Men felt uncomfortable around women who were manlier than them. Had no one taken her aside and taught her to act like a woman?

"My dad raised my three brothers and me. I've never had a female influence. I'm sure it hasn't gotten past you that I'm a dude with tits and a vagina."

"Are you happy with that?"

"Yes. No. I don't know." She drank her wine and refilled her glass. "I'm lonely, and I'm tired of paying to get a man to spend time with me. How do you think that makes a woman feel?"

"Probably the same as it makes me feel to take money for what I do." I'd always considered myself a commodity. Once my emotions were turned off, I was a thing to be bought and sold.

"I've never thought of you guys feeling anything about what you do except satisfied."

"I'm looking at you, Diane, and you have a lovely smile and the most feminine voice, but it's in stark contrast to the man clothes you wear. You don't have to be like a man to keep up with the men. Intimidation is most effective when you're a woman and can command the attention of men with your presence. Are you opposed to changing your style as an experiment?" I hoped she would say yes. I'd love to take this woman shopping. If there was one thing I knew after all this time, it was women's clothes and bodies.

She looked at me like she was searching for my motive. All I wanted to do was get through this night and see her smile again.

She put down the glass of wine she'd emptied and nodded her head.

"Is that a yes? If so, we're going to eat and then dash to some of my favorite stores. Tonight, the old Diane will take her final bow, and the new Diane will emerge."

"You sound like a television host unveiling the prize behind curtain number three."

"No, inside you is a beautiful woman waiting to spring free." God, I hoped I was right. Who knew, though? The boxy cut of her suit hid her body, and the severe cut of her hair did nothing to accentuate her eyes. If I really looked at them, they were pretty. They were brown with flecks of amber and gold. She needed more than a wardrobe.

We ate our dinner and flagged down a cab. The stores I loved in Soho were open until ten, so we had time to shop.

"What's our budget?"

"You sound like Rachel Zoe. Let's not go crazy, but we have plenty of money."

I offered her my hand and helped her from the cab when we pulled in front of Zip. It was a hip place that made clothes for women of all ages. Their claim to fame was how they used zippers. I loved the edginess of their designs, and a well-placed zipper was sexier than hell.

When we entered, I could have sworn Diane stopped breathing. I took her by the arm and sat her in the husband chair. "You sit here, I'll find some things that will look fabulous on you." With the help of a saleswoman, we rounded up several outfits for Diane to try on. She said she was a size eight, which was hard to believe given the clothes she wore.

I waited outside while she tried on the first dress. It was a little black number that zipped up the front. It was simple and elegant. Paired with a sweater or jacket, she could go from boardroom to bedroom in a flash.

"I'm not coming out." Her voice quivered.

"Bullshit, I want to see you." I shook the door until she opened the latch. "Holy shit, you have a freaking hot body." Her breasts were pushed together by the design of the dress. I tugged at the zipper to show more cleavage. "Who would have known you were hiding those under your sports coat?" I looked down at her sensible loafers and shook my head. "Those have to go."

"What? They're comfy." She pulled the zipper back up, and I tugged it down while I called for the saleslady and asked for heels.

"Hasn't a friend or a relative talked to you about fashion? Comfy isn't going to get you laid."

"No, money is."

"Well, let's see if we can change that." I would certainly give her what she was paying for, but her life would be infinitely better if she met someone who made her feel like Mim made me feel.

Thirty minutes later, we left Zip with two bags of clothes. I insisted she wear the black dress and heels because I had every intention of proving to her that she could attract a man. She stopped dead in her steps when I tried to pull her into Ulta. Clothes were fine, but this wasn't a naturally beautiful woman like Mim. Diane would need a little help.

"You're not stopping at the clothes. You're not going to

get made up to work the streets, but a little blush and lipstick will do you a world of good, and your eyes would pop with some liner and mascara."

She reluctantly followed me into the store. She was still getting used to the heels, so I had her hold my arm for balance while she tottered across the room.

"Can I help you?" A saleswoman named Tita approached us with a look of exactly how I felt. She scanned Diane and took her from me. "Oh honey, we have to make your face match your outfit. You can't go out looking like your face stayed in bed and your body got its groove on." Tita looked at me and said, "Give me thirty minutes." She opened her eyes wide and crossed her fingers behind Diane's back.

They walked toward the back of the store. I could hear Tita gush over the dress right before she asked Diane what barber she used. I wanted to laugh because the woman was spot on. While they did whatever women did, I looked around the store and found a small present I could afford. It was a jeweled purse mirror. I was pretty sure Diane didn't have anything like it.

Half an hour later, the new, much improved Diane walked forward. She didn't look confident, but she did seem eager.

"Wow." Tita had slicked Diane's hair back and spiked the top giving her an edgy look that went well with the dress. "You look fabulous." Compared to how she looked at dinner, she had taken a one hundred and eighty degree turn. She looked like a female. I loved the way her eyes shined as she soaked in the compliment.

"I feel like I'm wearing someone else's skin." She walked toward me, and I proudly held out my arm. Outside, the wind had picked up, making it a little chilly. I removed my jacket and hung it around her shoulders. Tears fell down her cheeks.

"What's wrong?" Had I gone too far? Had I pushed her too much?

"You putting your jacket around my shoulders was the nicest gesture I've ever received." She acted like I'd presented her with a two-carat diamond. I was just being me. I didn't have to think about giving her my jacket; the action was embedded in my DNA.

I stepped in front of her and brushed her tears with the pads of my thumbs. "You can't go ruining your makeup. We're going dancing." I pulled the tiny, jeweled mirror from my pocket and placed it in her hand. "Diane, I bought you this so you can see yourself as I see you. You look lovely tonight." I leaned down and kissed her cheek.

"You're going to make me cry again."

"You can't because then everyone will think I'm a louse for causing your tears."

"I don't dance."

"You do tonight."

She looked down at her watch. "We're over your time." She'd booked me for two hours, but in the grand scheme of things, it didn't really matter.

"The rest of the night is on me."

We walked the short block to Sway—a salsa club just blocks from my house. The distinctive Latin music filled the building. Once we dropped her bags at the coat check, I bought her a glass of wine and watched while she took in the scene. Bodies moved along the dance floor. Some just danced, while others looked like they were making love. Salsa was sexy and seductive, and the perfect place for Diane to find her inner deity.

I pulled the glass from her hand and led her kicking and complaining all the way to the dance floor. When I pulled her tightly to the front of my body, she shut up altogether.

"Just feel the rhythm." I swayed my hips to the beat. Pressing my hand against her lower back, I'd crushed her into my pelvis, giving her no option but to move with me. "Let the rhythm soak into your soul." She looked around at the people near us, worry or fear covering her face. "Shut your eyes; no one exists but you and me." I moved her around the dance floor several times. She never opened her eyes, but her smile told me something had changed for her tonight. I was going to have to thank River.

At eleven o'clock, I put a smiling Diane in a cab and sent her home. As far as work "dates" went, this was by far one of the most enjoyable I'd had in a while ... and to think, I would have chosen smallpox over a date with Diane months ago. I stepped out of my comfort zone and went the extra mile to make someone happy, and that felt good. I rubbed the worn side of my coin and smiled. Things were looking up.

When I got home, I texted Mim.

You make me happy. I miss you.

Love, Luca

Several minutes went by with no reply. I readied myself

for bed. When my phone beeped, I spat out the toothpaste and ran for it.

I was just falling asleep, hoping for a wet dream about you.

Love, Mim

I loved that we had graduated to ending our messages with affection.

Sorry to wake you. Go back to sleep and dream, baby.

Love, Luca xoxo

She must have dozed because I didn't hear back from her. I fell asleep wishing that I'd dream about Mim and the way her breast fit perfectly in my hand. The way her palm felt sliding over my hardness. The way I knew it would feel when I finally made love to her.

Chapter 10

It was just before nine, and I was at Mim's door with tea and a smile. I wanted to spend every moment we could together. She had managed to wind herself around my heart, and I needed her like I needed air. She was the only thing that made sense in my crazy world, and yet nothing about her or us made sense.

She let me in the door and walked me upstairs. Her eyes drooped from sleepiness, and her hair lay in tangles, but I'd never seen anything more stunning in my life. Every time I saw her, I fell a little more in love with her, making me want her so much. We'd hugged, and kissed, and cuddled, and even though she'd indicated she wanted more, I always made some excuse to leave when things became a bit too hot. She had started to call me altar boy, a nickname far from the truth.

Today, I escaped with the lame excuse that she had papers to grade for Saunders and I had a phone call to make.

I kissed her on the doorstep and bounced with happiness to the subway. I was ticking off my debt by thousand-dollar increments. My girlfriend was amazing, and there was an end in sight to the job I loathed.

When I pulled my graph from the closet last night, I checked off several thousand dollars. It was down to the wire, and I was determined to hit the zero mark before I was through.

My phone rang just as I'd made it to the third floor.

"Hi, Mom." She was better than an alarm.

"How was church, Luca?" Hope filled her voice.

"I didn't go, Mom. I took hot tea to my girlfriend, and we spent the morning together."

There was an eerie silence on her end.

"Girlfriend?" She made a happy squeak. "Oh, Luca, when are you going to bring her home to meet us?" Every weekend, she went on about the importance of faith, but at the mention of a girlfriend, she completely switched gears. "Tell me everything about her. Is she Italian? Catholic? Smart? Pretty?" She rattled off attributes like they were options to purchase.

"Not Italian, but she's Catholic, she's beautiful, and yes, she's smart, but it's too early to bring her home to the family. Besides, I have a lot to do before I graduate. I can't come back right now, Mom."

"Maybe we can come and see you soon?"

She must have covered the phone because I could hear muffled voices in the background. She was probably telling Dad she wanted to go to New York, but there was no risk of that happening. He liked to keep several states between his greatest disappointment and himself. It had been over a year since I'd seen my parents, but I couldn't imagine them jumping on a plane simply because I'd confessed to having a girlfriend.

After I'd hung up, I dove back into research. I'd fallen into a rhythm of sorts. I saw Mim every moment I could, and I showed up to work feeling less stressed and more motivated.

On Monday when I went to Laura Prater's office, I glanced out the window. My stomach roiled knowing somewhere across the street, in another high-rise, a man was finding his pleasure because of what I was giving his girlfriend. The thought made me angry; how could a man stand and watch his woman with another?

What used to be my easy job had now become one more thing I hated about this business. I'd been very clear about public sex on my job application. I didn't go there, and this was breaking all the rules. The fact that I didn't know it had been happening made it worse. My skin crawled, but I needed this job to reach my goal. This time, I pressed her against the window and took her from behind, where I hoped her perverted boyfriend's eyes couldn't see me.

Twofer Tuesday was fine. I went to Meredith's house, and we did our thing, only this time, she removed her shirt and insisted on a little foreplay before the main course. When I was holding her after, she told me something I'd never asked her, and she'd never divulged before, the reason she didn't have sex.

"I don't have intercourse because it scares the hell out of me." Her confession came out of the blue.

"Scares you?" There were a lot of reasons to fear sex, and I wasn't sure I wanted to dig deeper into hers, but something about the vulnerability in her eyes made me ask, "Why?"

She curled into a ball and sighed. "I've had two experiences. Both horrible." She snuggled against my shirt. "Rape at my high school prom, and after years of therapy, I let down my guard to allow a man in my life that wasn't worthy. He seduced me, and once we had awful sex, he moved on."

I rose up on my elbow and stared at the woman I'd known to be strong and capable, but not the least bit vulnerable. "What made it awful sex?" Was it truly awful, or did the memory of her rape taint the experience?

"It was painful in every sense of the word." She leaned back onto the emerald green spread that matched her eyes. "That's when I decided to hire someone to give me pleasure, not pain."

I pulled her to my side and held her for minutes. She didn't cry; she just let me hold her.

"Sex doesn't have to be that way," I whispered over her head. "You have a say in what you want. Relationships require honesty and openness." Here I was talking about being open and honest when my girlfriend knew nothing about what I did. I was too ashamed to tell her. "The next time you date a man, tell him the truth about your experiences and ask him to guide you through it. If he doesn't, he isn't worth your time." I felt like a heel giving out advice I refused to live by.

"What about you, Luca? Would you be willing to guide me through it?" She pulled out of my arms and watched me.

Damn it. I liked the clients who didn't want to use my dick. They somehow made me feel like less of a whore and more of a therapeutic assignment, but these women paid me to give them what they wanted. They were the clients, and I was in no position to say no.

"Yes, I work for you, Meredith, and whatever you want, you get." *Within reason.* However, lately, I was finding the line I'd drawn between absolute no and reasonable a bit gray. No public sex—unless, of course, you can hide in a high-rise and only have one man in an audience. No lying, unless it's to your girlfriend or your family and they're none the wiser. I shuddered to think of how low I'd sunk.

Thankfully, Shelby didn't want to pile on anything new to our arrangement, she was pissed at her brother, so we snuck into his garage and had sex in his Mustang, Shelby, 350 GT. It's a shit place to have sex, but Shelby was smiling when we left, and she put a few extra hundreds into my palm when I went home.

Being on-call for Sandra meant anything could pop up on my calendar, so seeing my Wednesday booked again didn't surprise me. Seeing Judith Kent's name did. She sent a car for me, and at six o'clock I arrived at her Long Island home. She lived on a large, sprawling estate in Oyster Bay.

I stood in front of the imposing wood doors and rang the

bell. I expected a butler or servant to answer, but the spry octogenarian I'd met last week greeted me.

"Come in, Luca." Judith moved to the side and waved me in. She was dressed in a black and purple pantsuit with enough amethysts to weigh her down. Judith obviously loved her jewelry.

I leaned in and kissed her weathered cheek just above the bright red blush that didn't get blended. "Judith, it's good to see you again. I'm surprised, though; I thought I was a one-date wonder." I followed her into a yellow room decorated with flowers and vines.

"Oh, the girls just loved you, and I needed to have some new fodder to tell those old biddies." She spoke of her friends as if they were ancient and she was newborn.

"Fodder?" I was rarely slow on the uptake, but talking to Judith was like solving a puzzle.

"Yes, I thought if you came over and organized one of my kitchen drawers, I could tell them you were in my drawers." She laughed until the remainder of her skin matched her blush.

"You hired me to come over and clean out your drawers?" This was a first for me.

"Of course. Did you think I wanted you to ravish me? Dear Lord, I could imagine it now. I'd be in traction until my death." She walked over to a scotch decanter and poured us both a drink. "When you get my age, Luca, you have to find the things that tickle you. Telling my friends you had your fingers in my drawers is fun."

I thought I'd experienced everything up until that

moment. "Judith, let me see your drawers so I can make an honest woman out of you."

I followed her into her kitchen, where she opened her silverware drawer. Not a thing was out of place.

She squinted her eyes and pursed her lips. "I thought my spoons and forks should be switched." Those pursed lips spread into a grin. "Yes, that should do it."

I picked up the forks and spoons and switched their places. Job done. Now what? "I don't feel right about charging you for this date, Judith."

"Oh, nonsense. I have more money than sense. Let an old lady have some fun. In fact, I was hoping we could meet weekly until your contract is up. I like you, and I think you have a good heart. It's not often you meet people who want more for you than themselves."

I didn't know where she got that impression, I'd been doing everything I could to push my agenda for the last two years. "I'm not that good of a person. Look at what I do for a living, Judith."

"It's honest work, right?"

"I wouldn't say it's honest. I'm ashamed of myself most of the time, but I see the light at the end of the tunnel." *That was honest.*

"Let me tell you a story." She carried her drink to the living room and sat on the floral sofa. I slumped into the chair across from her. "I was born in 1932. The country was just starting to recover from the 1928 stock market crash. Hundreds of thousands of people were jobless, hungry, and destitute. Do you think I grew up in luxury?" She sipped at her drink and looked around her swanky home. "I grew up in Kansas in the middle of the dust bowl. I know what desperation looks like. By the time I was fourteen, I was done with it all."

"What did you do?"

"I packed up and moved to New York. I got a fancy outfit, a cute pair of shoes, and I put myself in front of the richest bachelors in the United States." Her eyes sparkled with mischief. "What you did and what I did aren't much different. I sold my entire self to one man, while you sell bits and pieces to many."

"I wouldn't call them bits, Judith," I teased. "Tell me about Mr. Kent."

"He was an Astor by blood on his mother's side. Lots of old money but mostly in shipping, and hotels. Not a dime was actually his. My Winston wanted to make a name for himself, so he went the way of finance. Once he earned enough to invest in himself, he built Kent International, which mines precious stones." She fingered the amethysts hanging from her neck. "Every piece of jewelry I have comes from one of our mines."

"Wow." I'd never considered using finance as a stepping stone into another field. It was the end all, be all for me. "How did you get involved in The Dean's List?"

"That's easy. When my Winston was over in Africa at the Prosperity Diamond Mine, I was bored and entered the school as a way to spend my time. I majored in finance, thinking I could help Winston out when he was out of the country. I'm a generous donor to the school, and when I need arm candy, I call Sandra."

"That was bold of you."

"Do I look like a fading rose to you?" She rolled her blue-shadowed eyes. "Winston married me because I convinced him I was an asset, and I proved I was. While he traveled from mine to mine, I ran his business like Satan with a bouffant. I tripled his earnings in the first year." Judith's voice took on a dreamy tone. "Until his dying day, he always told me I was his most precious gem."

"Do you regret not having children?"

She appeared to ponder my question for a moment. "No, Winston and I had each other and our careers, and that was enough. He's been gone for ten years now, and I fill my life with people who intrigue me."

"I intrigue you?"

"Yes, because you're not who you appear to be. I'm not even sure you know who you are, but I do."

I sipped at the scotch and watched as Judith analyzed me. "Who am I?"

"Oh, Luca, you are so much more than you think."

She didn't elaborate. She pulled me into the kitchen, where we ate cold smoked salmon and cheese. Two hours later, the car picked me up. We had agreed to meet next week at six, where we would barbecue chicken. I told her she could tell her friends I was coming over to massage her breasts … chicken breasts, that was.

Judith Kent was more than I could have hoped for in a

companion. She was wise and witty, and something told me I'd learn a lot about myself in her presence.

My week ended with my second date with Diane. We did a bit more shopping and then went to a movie. She was going for the boyfriend experience. She hadn't asked me to have sex with her yet, and that was fine with me. I would be happy if that never happened. She did try to kiss me once, but I laid out the ground rules. I never kissed clients, except on the cheek. She didn't seem happy, but she didn't press me for more.

Chapter 11

Sunday began at a diner with Mim. She loved hash and eggs, and I was happy to find her the places that specialized in her favorite. We snuggled in a booth and stole kisses. I'd never done so little with a woman and been so completely satisfied. My dick and I had an understanding: as long as it performed on demand, it would be rewarded with Mim down the road. In all honesty, it rose every time I saw her, but my brain was finally in control of the situation. I knew what had to be done or not done for my relationship with Mim to grow in its purest form.

We spent the afternoon at her place. I helped with her laundry while she graded more papers. "I should get extra points for my assignment since you're making me fold your underwear." I stood by the couch, where I'd dumped her load of clean laundry.

She sat at her kitchen table with papers spread all over.

"I'm grading you harder because you're my boyfriend. I don't want to be accused of favoritism." She bit into a Jaffa Cake. The orange jelly oozed from the corner of her lip.

"That's not fair." I picked up her pink barely there panties and folded them into a tiny parcel. It was too bad I had to fold her laundry to get close to her panties.

She washed down the little cake and licked the remaining jelly from her lip. "Come and kiss me. I'll make it up to you."

I left the clothes lying on her sofa and went to her. "You can be as hard on me as you want, as long as I'm rewarded." My lips melted into hers, and all thoughts of folding laundry or grading papers were gone. She pulled me toward her room, but I stilled in the hallway. "Oh shit, look at the time." After a cursory glance at my watch, I released Mim and raced around her house, collecting my stuff. "I gotta go. I'll be here in the morning to pick you up for school." In a flash, I was out her door and racing down the steps. I flew past her father so fast, he didn't have time to set his face in a scowl.

When I was a block away, my pace slowed. I didn't have anywhere to be, but I couldn't end up in Mim's bed. I'd have to figure out a way to keep us out of her house, and mine.

Mom called at one and was disappointed with my lack of religious enthusiasm, but she seemed satisfied when I mentioned Mim and how we'd spent the morning together again.

Monday morning, I was standing in front of Mim's when she walked out. "Are you sure you have time to go to school?"

I knew she was miffed at me for leaving without a word, but it was self-preservation. "I had a hair appointment." My first out-and-out lie to her.

She ran her fingers through my hair. "You're not getting your money's worth. It looks exactly the same."

"I'm told that's the sign of a good cut. Besides, I needed a good conditioning." I pulled whatever excuse I could from my ass.

"Are you sure you're into women?" She twisted her fingers with mine and walked with me to the subway.

"Absolutely. Would I kiss you like I do if I weren't?"

"Maybe."

"I'm definitely not a guy who likes men. I'm cool with those who do, but I'm all for girls. Not just any girl, but my girl."

I squeezed her hand in mine. I was getting the feeling that if I didn't show her something sooner, she'd continue to doubt my manhood. This whole situation was comical. I proved my manliness several times a week, but when it came to the girl I was falling for, I couldn't do a damn thing to convince her of my prowess. The world was unfair.

After class, I worked out at the gym and then went to see Laura Prater. I was less than enthusiastic this time. I unzipped my pants and did what she wanted. I collected my hour and went on my way.

Tuesday night had me sweating in my loafers. I showed up at Meredith's house, not knowing what to expect. She was just a job before, but now she was more. She wanted me to guide her into sex. I wasn't a therapist; I was a gigolo.

I felt like I was sixteen again in the basement of my house, getting my first feel of Darla Darian's boobs, except this time there was no excitement. I was terrified. Tonight had nothing to do with sex, but everything to do with compassion. I wasn't sure I had what it would take to get me through this evening, or what Meredith would need to get her through her crisis.

I poured us both a glass of wine, unusual for me. We sipped our drinks and talked for a few minutes before Meredith led me to her room.

On the nightstand, I spied a candle, which I lit to help with the ambiance. Maybe making the evening more of a date than a clinical trial would help things. Nope, a date was the wrong thought; the only person I dated was Mim.

"Do you want me to stay mostly dressed?" I needed some guidance, too. Did she want the full body on body routine, or just me taking her through the motions?

"Treat me like you'd treat a woman you wish to make love to."

The need in her voice twisted my heart. The guilt I felt warped my gut. Here I was getting ready to fulfill the need of a woman I didn't love, when the needs of the one I did went unmet.

My mouth was dry, and my hands began to sweat. I'd brought this woman to orgasm more times than I could count, and now I was nervous? I chastised myself silently and started to peel off her clothes like I had many times before. She lay naked in the glow of the candlelight.

I pulled my jacket off first and followed it with my shirt. Standing in my trousers, I toed off my shoes and pulled my socks free. This was as bare as I'd ever been with Meredith.

"You are a handsome man, Luca. Someday, some woman is going to be so lucky. Tonight, it's going to be me."

The pressure was on. I unbuckled my belt and let my pants drop. I wasn't hard; in fact, I wasn't sure I could get hard, but I'd do my best to make Meredith happy.

Up her body, I slid. Her heart raced; I could see it in the pulse of the vein I licked at her neck. I ran my tongue down across her shoulder blades and lowered my attention to her breasts. Still, in my black underwear, I kneeled between her legs and worshiped her body the best way I knew how. I was methodical, going for the erogenous zones first—her ears, her neck, her breasts. I slid to the floor and ran my tongue from her ankles to the inside of her thighs. I could smell her arousal. It wasn't the scent that turned me on, but this wasn't about me. I pulled the rubber barrier from her drawer and placed it on her sex. With heated swipes, I worked her into a passionate frenzy, and when I stroked her with a single finger, she stiffened.

"Relax, Meredith. You hold all the power. All you have to do is say no or stop." I dipped my head down and continued to bring her pleasure while slowly pressing my first finger into her hot sex.

I knew she had relaxed when her legs lost their tension

and fell to the sides. That's when I slid the second finger inside. She paused briefly, but her passion didn't dim.

"Shit, Luca. That feels incredible." She panted and squirmed beneath me. "I want more."

I had hoped I could fulfill her wish with my tongue and fingers, but Meredith had her mind set on the real deal. "Are you sure? Maybe we should go slow." I hoped she would change her mind.

"Shut up. I'm forty-four years old, and I've had sex twice. I have a lot of catching up to do." She rocked her hips toward me. "I feel safe with you."

I reached into my pants and stroked myself until I became hard. Not stone hard, but usable hard. I stood up and pulled off my underwear. She watched every move I made. After reaching for the condom, I asked if she wanted to put it on or have me do it. She looked appalled, so I took that as a no.

I climbed between her thighs and lined myself up. "Are you sure?" I asked again. She nodded.

I pressed gently into her. A fraction of an inch was all I dared. She scrunched her eyes closed.

"It's Luca, not anyone else. You know me. You know I'd never hurt you." An inch more, and I heard her gasp. "This is us, Meredith, giving pleasure to one another, like you wanted." I pressed deeper, and she shook. "I can pull out. Nothing says we have to continue." I leaned in and kissed her neck, and when I got to her ear, I said, "You control me."

She breathed in and out rapidly. I braced myself over her and began to slide out of her.

"Don't you dare. If I don't go through with this, I'll die a sexless spinster." She gripped my hips and stopped me from retreating. "Please, Luca, make me feel something other than fear."

"What are you feeling now?" I sank into her inch by inch until I was fully seated.

"Full."

"Are you in pain?"

"Yes, but not how you'd think. I hurt because I gave up something as beautiful as this because someone was so ugly to me." Tears ran down her cheeks.

"Move with me, sex is a team sport."

I slid in and out of her slowly. I watched her face for any indication she wanted me to stop, but her eyes never showed another glimpse of doubt. They glowed with years of pent-up passion. Her hips rocked with mine. Her moans built into a crescendo until her body shook, and her voice whispered incoherent words. I could feel her pulse around me in wave after wave of untethered passion, and for the first time in my life, I faked an orgasm. I wasn't interested in my own release. I had given her what she needed, and my job was done.

Chapter 12

The next few weeks passed like a bullet train. I counted the time by Sundays with Mim and Wednesdays with Judith.

I approached the table at Leland's Steakhouse with a bit of trepidation. Tonight, Mim and I were dining with her parents. In any other circumstance I would have been fine eating with the parents, but given Marcus Knight's dislike for me, I was nervous.

Mim jumped up from the booth and threw her arms around my neck. She had no inhibitions. Even with her father present, she was getting her kiss. She pressed her lips to mine and tried to get me to deepen the kiss by opening her mouth and offering the sweetness of her tongue, but I pulled back after a quick kiss and helped her back into the booth. I was like salt on Marcus' open wound, and any display of affection beyond a kiss wouldn't have been right.

"Good evening, Mr. Knight—Mrs. Knight." I looked at both parents and smiled. "Thanks for inviting me to dinner." Mrs. Knight smiled, while her husband grumbled under his breath.

"Luca, it's so lovely to be able to spend some quality time with you," Mim's mom said.

I slid into the booth next to Mim and placed my palm on her thigh. "Yes, it will be nice to get to know you better." I looked directly at Mim's father. "To have you know me better." I wanted Marcus to know me. He had a preconceived notion of who I was by what I did.

We ordered a bottle of wine with dinner and enjoyed light conversation. Several times during the meal, Mim would take my hand and force it farther up her thigh. When I could finally make love to her, she was going to pay for all the times she'd teased me. I leaned in and whispered in her ear, "Behave." She giggled and continued to talk while she changed her tactic and rubbed her hand up my thigh to my hardening length.

Damn her.

"Tell me, Luca," Georgina Knight said, "do you attend church?" She hugged her husband's arm and leaned her head against his shoulder. I could picture Mim and me in the same position thirty years from now. Mim was everything I would ever want.

"Mum," Mim piped in, "he's basically an altar boy."

I choked on my wine. "I'm not an altar boy, but I was raised Catholic—although, in all honesty, I haven't made much time for church lately." I looked at Marcus, and he seemed pleased. Maybe knowing his daughter thought I was an altar boy pleased him. "I've been talking to a local priest, and he's doing his best to coax me back to his flock."

"Mim says you have a few weeks of school left, and I was thinking that having a quiet place to contemplate one's life would be a good thing."

Marcus white-knuckled the edge of the table.

"I'll keep that in mind. The next few weeks will be stressful." I glared at Marcus. "I will be wrapping up things at my current job. They only hire college students, so I have to move on. I'm hoping to land a few interviews. Life will be busy for a bit."

"Mim says you work at a concierge service. What's that like?" She leaned forward and tuned into my every word. It was obvious her husband hadn't shared my real profession, and for that I was grateful. I hoped it showed in the look of gratitude I shot Marcus.

"It's different all the time. My job is to give the clients what they want." I lowered my eyes, not wanting to see the disgust in Marcus'.

"That sounds interesting," Georgina said.

"It can be."

Nothing else was said on the subject. We ate our dinners and shared desserts. When the bill came, I tried to pay, but Marcus insisted he pay, saying I would need every dollar I earned. After we'd helped the women into their jackets, Marcus tugged me to the side.

"In spite of what you do, I believe you are a good man, Luca. Prove me right." He thumped me on my back the way a father would. Somehow, I might have earned a little respect from Mim's dad.

"Let's go to your place. You have proper tea, right?" Mim asked.

She knew I did. I'd purchased every brand of English tea I could find. Turns out, PG Tips was her favorite. She loved those with Walkers shortbread cookies. If anyone looked in my pantry, they would assume an English chap lived there. I had Hobnobs, and Cadbury, Jammie Dodgers, and Jaffa cakes. I bought anything I thought would make Mim happy.

Once in my apartment, she pulled me into the bedroom. "Luca Gregorio, you are going to have sex with me. I've never waited so long with anyone." She walked to the bed and began to strip. God, she was beautiful. I wanted her so much, but I couldn't have her. Not yet. "You're starting to make me think you're a virgin, but I'm willing to pop your cherry."

I shouldn't have laughed, but the thought of her popping my cherry was hysterical. By the time I calmed down, she was naked but not happy with me, and all I wanted to do was please her. She made me want to be a better man.

Her beauty stunned me. I'd felt her breasts and cupped her ass a few times, but I'd never seen her stripped and standing gloriously nude before me. The sight of her willingly gifting herself to me sucked the air from the room. I felt dizzy. I felt drunk. I felt completely in love.

"Come to bed, Luca." Her voice was like the purr of a cat, soft and sensuous. "Please."

"Mim, I can't." I stared at her loveliness, and my heart ached.

She stared at the outline straining against my pants. "You can. I can see that you can."

My resistance was fading. My mouth was watering. My need was too great. I walked toward her and fell to my knees. Anyone that beautiful should be revered. I argued, telling myself I couldn't, but I knew I would. My internal turmoil was too great. I bargained with myself. I could touch her, but not have her. I could taste her, but not press myself inside of her, I could . . . I could . . . I couldn't.

I kissed her stomach and ran my tongue from hip to hip. I cupped her bottom and pulled her close. The feel of her body in my hands was heaven. I'd touched many women, but I was touching Mim with my heart. Every caress came from a place deep inside—a place that loved her beyond everything.

She angled herself toward the bed and fell onto the mattress. It was too much temptation not to follow. I explored her body, starting at her feet. She had perfect toes, all painted pink. Her smooth legs flexed under my hands as I traveled upwards. Her thighs fell apart to allow me access. I buried my face between her legs and inhaled her scent. *It was heaven.* I followed the finely trimmed patch to her sweet spot and slid my tongue along her crease. She moaned and pulled at my hair. I climbed up her body and lingered at her breasts. Her hardened nipples reached for my mouth, their pink buds screaming for attention. I pulled one against the heat of my tongue and sucked, rolling it between my lips before I relinquished it.

She rose from the bed. "God, Luca, what's taken you so long?" Her hands frantically reached for the buttons of my shirt. She tore at the material until it pulled free.

I shrugged out of it and pressed my naked chest against hers. Every fiber of my being ignited. She tugged at my pants, but I pulled her arms over her head and pinned them there. I had to get control of this situation. If I didn't, I'd never be able to look at her again.

"Mim, look at me." She opened her eyes, and I swear her oceans of blue swallowed me whole. I was drowning in lust and love. "I love you, Mim." Once the words were out, I couldn't stop them. "I love you more than you can imagine, and because I love you, I can't have you just yet."

"No, God, Luca, look at me, I'm throwing myself at you. Don't leave me like this." She buried her face in her hands and began to cry.

"Baby, I'm not leaving. I'm never leaving." I pulled her hands from her face and covered her mouth with mine. It broke my heart that I couldn't give her everything she wanted, but I could give her something. I lay next to her and told her how much I loved her. Then I made love to her with my mouth. I covered her breasts one at a time and pulled the taut peaks across my heated tongue.

When I slipped my hand between her legs, she sighed. It was the sweetest sound. I hadn't brought her to orgasm, but her sound of satisfaction drove me forward. She was wet, and I was so damn hard for her, I hurt. It would be so easy to drop my pants and find equal satisfaction between her thighs, but I owed her all of me, and I couldn't give her that if

I were sharing that part of myself with others. She deserved nothing less than everything.

She groaned when I slid a finger into her heat. She began grinding her hips into my hand when I followed with the second. Her breath hitched, and she tensed. The minute I thumbed her tight little button, her hips rose from the bed and I felt her insides pulse against my fingers. I caressed her down from the high and pulled her naked body into my arms.

"I love you, Luca." Those words harnessed my heart so tightly, I thought I'd die. She loved me. Her breathing slowed to an even pace, and minutes later she was asleep.

I slowly pulled myself away from her and covered her with my comforter. She was so beautiful lying in my bed, and I wanted her there always.

Chapter 13

The ringing of my phone woke me. The clock on the nightstand read six-thirty.

Who in the hell called at six thirty?

Mim stretched like a cat next to me while I answered the phone.

"Hello." When her arms stretched above her head, I leaned down and pulled her nipple into my mouth. She let out a hum that made me instantly hard.

The voice on the other end interrupting my first sleepover was my mom. Mim's nipple popped from my mouth. "What? You're where? Shit." I leaped from the bed and gathered Mim's clothes. With my hand over the receiver, I said, "Get dressed."

"Sorry, I wasn't expecting you. I'll be right down." I hung up the phone and let out a string of expletives that would make anyone blush.

"What's wrong?" Mim pulled on her dress and searched for her underwear, which were at the foot of the bed. "Who's here?" She slipped her legs into her panties and shimmied them up.

"My parents." I dragged my hand through my hair.

"Is it a problem that I'm here?" She sounded hurt.

I stopped and pulled her into my arms. "No, I just thought you might want to be dressed." I pressed a kiss to her forehead. "Time to meet the parents, and Mim, I meant what I said last night." I hopped on one foot to pull my socks and shoes on. "I love you."

I ran from the apartment and down the stairs. Why my parents decided to show up unannounced I had no idea.

When I reached the door, my father stood next to my mom with a stoic expression glued to his face. Mom was standing on the sidewalk with a small suitcase and a big smile.

"Surprise." Mom dropped her bag and closed her arms around me. A few minutes later, she was pinching my cheek and telling me how she needed to see her son.

"You could have called." I thought about Mim upstairs and wondered what my parents' reaction would be. They were devout Catholics, and premarital anything was taboo. "I'm not alone," I said as we reached the third floor. "Mim is here." Ever since I'd told Mom about Mim, she'd asked enough questions to satisfy a security clearance.

"Luca, you're not sleeping with her, are you?" How did my parents stay in the Dark Ages while the world rushed forward?

"Mom, it's the twenty-first century. People sleep together. Mim and I slept together, but we haven't had sex." Dad gave me a *don't-lie-to-your-mom* look. "She fell asleep, and I let her sleep."

Mom pulled her hands to her ears. "I don't want details." She proceeded to make *la la la* sounds until I opened the door.

Mim was in the kitchen, making tea for her and coffee for me. I tried to give her an *I'm sorry* look, but I'm not sure she got it. She walked over to my mom and hugged her, and within minutes they were talking like they'd known each other forever.

"Son, how are you?" Dad walked out of the kitchen, where Mom was peppering Mim with questions.

"I'm good, Dad, what about you?" We'd shared under a dozen words, and I was pretty sure that would be the extent of our conversation while he was here. He wasn't much of a talker.

"Fine." He sat on the couch and stared at the blank television.

I picked up the remote and turned on the news. When I was sure he was sufficiently entertained, I sought out the two women I loved the most. They were sitting at the small table in the kitchen, sipping tea.

I didn't know Mom drank tea.

"Luca, why didn't you tell me she was so pretty?" Mom sighed and looked at Mim with appreciation.

"I did, Mom. I said she was stunning right between your

questions of whether she was Catholic and if she was Italian." I'd made Mom blush.

"I'm Catholic, Mrs. Gregorio, but sadly, I'm not Italian, and I hope you won't hold that against me."

"Call me Stella, and that grump out there," she nodded toward the living room, "is Frank. I'll forgive you for not being Italian. We can't all be perfect." She patted Mim's hand like she was serious, and then she began to laugh. "You look just about perfect to me."

I stood against the counter and watched the two women talk. I had so much respect for Mim. She went from a dead sleep to meeting my mother in a second, and she was handling it like a champ.

"I have to go because I have to work, but I'd love to visit while you're here." Mim stood up and put her teacup in the sink. "Luca has to work tonight. Maybe I can come by and take you both out for a tour of the city."

Shit, I did have to work.

"If you'd given me some notice, I could have arranged to have the day off. It's too late now."

"Oh, that's okay. We knew we would only catch glimpses of you, but since we haven't seen you all year," she looked at me with sadness, "we felt it was worth it. I'd love it if you came by, Mim." Mom rose from her chair and put her teacup in the sink. "You two say goodbye. Luca and I will shop for dinner. Come by around five, Mim, and enjoy a real Italian meal."

Mim smiled at my mom and waved to my dad as she

walked by. "Walk me out?" She pulled on my hand, and I followed her out the door.

"I'm so sorry, Mim. I would have said something had I known." I ran my hands down her arms.

"Luca, your parents are nice. I'm so glad I got to meet them. Do you mind if I take them out tonight? I thought maybe I could take them to the theater. My dad always has unused tickets."

"They would love that, but I can get the tickets. I do work for a concierge service." Free tickets were one of the perks I never used. My clients were interested in one thing only, and that never happened at the theater.

We held hands and walked down the stairs. She only had a few minutes to pull herself together, but she looked like she'd worked on herself for hours. "You are the most beautiful woman I've ever met."

"Well, this woman just had to call in late because her boyfriend let her fall asleep in his arms, which was amazing, by the way." At the bottom of the steps, she pulled me into her embrace. Her purse dropped to the floor, and her copy of *The Scarlet Letter* spilled out.

"Luca, I wanted more last night. I wanted to give you something, too. I owe you." She reached up and kissed me.

"You don't owe me anything. Every minute with you is a gift. I'm so glad you were so rude to me our first day." I pushed the hair that had fallen over her face and nipped at her lip.

"I'll have to keep that in mind. Maybe being rude is foreplay for you."

"Baby, anything you do is like foreplay to me. You breathe in my direction, and I'm stiff."

"Yeah, yeah, all talk and no action." She reached down and picked up her book.

"How are things going for Hester? Will she find her happily ever after?" I took the book from her hands and scrolled through the pages until I came across a quote that caught my attention. *"No man for any considerable period can wear one face to himself and another to the multitude, without finally getting bewildered as to which may be true."* I shut the book and pressed it back into her hand.

"Hester learns to find happiness where she is. It's not perfect, but she has to find a way to live with herself, and she does. Happiness comes in many forms. Sometimes it's as simple as waking up in your arms."

Our goodbye kiss was soft and full of love. "Luca, I meant every word I said last night." She paused and reached up to brush her fingers across my cheek. "I love you."

My chest swelled with happiness. I knew when I got upstairs there would be a lot of questions to answer, and my mother didn't disappoint. Mom lobbed questions at me like a tennis pro. I volleyed every one. When she asked if Mim was the one, I didn't hesitate to say yes. She was the one, and I knew it in the deepest part of my dark soul. Without her, I'd be less.

My parents needed a place to sleep, so I pulled the sheets from my bed and brought them to my nose. They smelled of her, and I was reluctant to wash away her scent. How was I going to get through the next month without exploding?

Once the room was ready, we spent the remainder of the morning visiting Italian markets around town. Mom had her favorite brands, and it took three stores to locate what she wanted. Dad followed like any respectable Italian man. Men ruled the roost until it came to cooking; that particular task was left to the professionals—the women.

By one o'clock, we were back home and Mom was busy in the kitchen. Dad had returned to the couch to watch an old John Wayne movie.

My graduate project was looming over me and couldn't be put off any longer. It felt like I was home in Chicago doing homework while Mom cooked dinner. I hadn't realized how much I missed my family until now.

Dad was easy to overlook since he was mostly silent. It was in his non-silent moments that I didn't care much for him. He wasn't big on praise, but he was huge on expectation and letting me know how much I had disappointed him. I glanced toward the couch and caught a rare glimpse of him smiling. Something funny must have happened on the show. What I would do to see him smile at me with pride in his eyes just once.

"I like her, Luca. She's smart and kind, and she has good hips for babies." Mom rattled around my kitchen, complaining about my lack of quality pans. "She says her father is a reproductive specialist."

I looked at her, and in the reflection of her eyes I saw the grandchildren she hoped I'd give her.

"Mom, don't rush us. There can't be any grandbabies until there's sex, and there hasn't been any of that."

She ignored my comment and started chopping green peppers. When they left on Sunday, I'd have enough leftovers to last me for weeks. Thank God for plastic storage containers and freezer bags.

"I want to meet this priest you've been telling me about—this Father Tobin. You'll take us there for Mass, right?"

The *chop chop* of vegetables drowned out my groan. The last thing I wanted was to go to Mass and have Mary looking down at me like a disillusioned mother while the other saints mocked me with their silent stares.

I brought Dad a cold beer and went back to my project. I'd logged five years of stock history for the most successful and least successful companies trading on the exchange. I'd analyzed the data and ran the numbers. It wasn't rocket science, but I'd compiled substantial information on successes and failures. The only thing left to do was write the report, and I had three weeks to get that done.

TICKETS for The Lion King were delivered to will call. I was grateful to Mim for babysitting my parents tonight. I wouldn't have to worry about Mom reorganizing my apartment while I was at work. There were too many things that would raise her blood pressure. The case of condoms, for one, would give her a coronary. Imagine if she found my testing results for STDs.

By five, I had showered and trimmed up my facial hair.

My mother hated it, but Mim loved it, and she won. Scruff, she called it, every time she rubbed her cheek against it.

What I wanted to do was call off tonight and join my family, but the end was in sight, and Jessica was easy. Feeling a bit glum, I dressed in gray to match my mood and went to the kitchen.

"Look at my fancy boy. So handsome in his suit." Mom ran her fingers down the lapel and smiled. "Nice. How do you afford such nice things?"

"In New York, you can find anything you want if you look hard enough. Even a cheap suit looks good when tailored."

I took off my jacket and laid it over a chair, hiding the label. It was an Armani suit, and although Mom knew quality when she saw it, she didn't know brands. Dad didn't make enough to afford brands like Armani or Hugo Boss. They stuck to stores like Kohl's and Target.

Mim called to say she was downstairs, and I flew out the door to let her in. My door buzzer wasn't working, so any guests had to be let in personally. I didn't mind. It would give me a few minutes to spend alone with her.

She looked a bit frazzled when I opened the door. Her brow was glistening with sweat, and tendrils of damp hair stuck to her forehead. "I ran from the station because I didn't want your mother to think me inconsiderate by being late."

"My mom has already fallen in love with you. She's been dreaming of her future grandchildren all day." I pushed her damp hair from her face and nibbled on her lower lip in the way she loved. She pulled me close and deepened the kiss. Our tongues danced together until we were breathless. "I missed you today. How was work?"

"It was good. Professor Saunders invited me to sit in on the graduate projects. Did you know you get fifty points for just showing up?" She bounced up and down like she'd won the lottery. "I get to see yours in person. I'm so excited."

"Nothing like putting the pressure on a poor grad student. At least if I show, I'm guaranteed an F."

"Yes, but it's fifty percent of your grade."

"You're full of news today." I laced my fingers through hers. "We should get upstairs. My mother has been cooking for hours. I hope you're hungry."

"I'm starving. I worked through lunch to make up for being late and leaving early." She rubbed her flat stomach. "I'm happy to eat until I get fat tonight."

I rubbed my hand across her bottom and grabbed her hips. "My mom thinks you have perfect hips for having babies. I think you have perfect hips for everything." At the front door, I kissed her passionately. The kiss would have to last until I got back from work.

I didn't pray much, but I prayed Jessica wanted a quick night. That would get me back before Mim and my parents returned from the theater.

"Tickets to The Lion King are waiting at will call for you." I rubbed her bottom. "Thanks for taking my parents."

When the door opened, Mim no longer belonged to me. She was whisked into the kitchen where my mom told her all about the dishes she made. Cooking was woman's work according to Mom, and I was smart enough to join Dad in the living room until we were summoned to the kitchen.

"Mangiare," Mom called out after she insisted we say grace.

Even though it was my house, dad was served first, and then the rest of us dug in. Mim ate like she'd been starved for days. I filled my plate with spaghetti and sausage and Mom's famous roasted peppers.

The conversation centered on the show they'd see tonight. I'd chosen well; Mim had never seen The Lion King. By six, I had to run. I needed to get to Fifth Avenue by seven. I kissed Mom, said goodbye to Dad, and tried to devour Mim in the hallway before I left.

I was ten steps outside the door when I texted her.

You drive me crazy with love . . . and lust.

Love you,

Luca

She responded a long five minutes later.

You make me crazy in general, but I love you. We're in the taxi and on our way. By the way, does your father ever smile?

I laughed out loud. My parents were a particular flavor she'd either love or hate. Thank God Mom's personality would outshine Dad's lack of one.

No, but he'll grow on you like mold. I'll make it up to you.

Hugs

I was just catching my train when her reply came through.

Hugs won't cut it this time. I'm expecting so much more. Don't work too hard.

Hugs for now.

Chapter 14

At seven o'clock, I walked into Jessica's apartment. She seemed frazzled and slightly disorganized. Her hair was pinned up, and she was still dressed in a suit. Immediately, I poured her a glass of wine and grabbed a soda for myself.

"Late day?" Without a thought, I took a seat on the couch and pulled her down next to me. She didn't lean into me like Mim did; she leaned away, kicked off her heels and plopped her feet in my lap.

Once I set my soda on the black lacquered table, I went right to work massaging the kinks out of her toes. Why did women insist on wearing such high heels to work? A lower heel would be more comfortable and still look good.

"I told you about the Singapore deal. I've been talking to my dad about it, and I think I'm going to do it." She pulled the pins out of her hair and let it fall across the soft velvet arm of the couch. The white of the material made an excellent backdrop for her dark hair.

"What made you decide to take the job?"

"You did." She rolled her neck and groaned as the vertebrae popped into place.

"Me?" I set her feet down and picked up my soda. "How?" We both pulled our legs in and turned toward each other.

"I started thinking about my life. It's unique, to say the least, and maybe it's time to make it more mainstream." She looked at the ceiling as if the answers to life's questions were there. "I want to make my mark in the world, and going out on my own is the only way. Until I get out from under my dad, no one will see what I bring to the table."

"You're incredibly smart and capable. I think it's a good choice for you." It seemed like everyone faced dilemmas and demons. Having money and options didn't diminish anything.

"What about you, Luca? What's in your future? We have a few weeks left, and then you're out of my life for good." She said the words in a good riddance way, but she was teasing. She valued the time we spent together.

"I'm still looking for a job. Things are going well with my girlfriend. She's amazing." I closed my eyes and pictured Mim standing naked in front of my bed. She'd exposed herself completely to me, and I'd hid everything from her.

"God, look at you. You get this wistful look on your face when you talk about her. Lord, you got it bad." She drank down the wine and handed the empty glass to me.

Like the paid servant I was, I got up and went to the bar

to get her a refill. "I can't argue with that," I said as I filled her glass with merlot. "I'm in love with her." I'd miss Jessica; she was real and someone I'd considered a friend in spite of the dynamics of our relationship. I felt protective of her, but then I felt protective of all women. I was raised in the same way most Italian boys were raised. There was a certain machismo that came with the last name Gregorio, but despite my cockiness, I was brought up to revere women.

"How do you show up for your appointments and perform knowing there's a woman pining for you at home while you swing your dick around? It doesn't matter how you justify what you do, it's still cheating." Typical Jessica, just laid it all out there.

"Honestly, I've compartmentalized my work so much that it feels like another person goes to work and Luca stays home. It's a job. I don't pretend to be anything but a dick for hire."

"Oh please, you are so much more than what hangs between your legs. I bet every woman who hires you talks your ear off. You're a woman's man. They like you because you listen."

"No, some women just want to get nailed, and I'm good at that, too. Although you would never know." I mentally ran through my regulars in my head, and Jessica was right. Most of the women wanted some kind of validation. Hell, I'd seen Diane for over a month, and we'd never had sex. She wanted to feel like a woman, and I gave her that. "Why haven't we ever had sex?" Did she have similar hang-ups to Meredith?

"It's not that I have an aversion to penis. The problem is,

they can't vibrate like a jackhammer or twirl like a top. Then there's the size, although yours is impressive, even you can't beat the length and girth of my favorite toy."

There was no denying it. One of her favorites would make porn legend Ron Jeremy feel inadequate.

"Speaking of toys, are you ready?" It wasn't my intent to rush her, but I wanted to be home when Mim and my parents got back from the theater.

"Girlfriend waiting at home?" She lifted her eyes before she rose from the couch and walked to her room.

"No, my parents showed up unexpectedly, and she took them to a show, but I'd like to be home when they get home."

She stripped out of her suit and pulled a toy from her nightstand. I took my position standing between her legs, and we both did what we do. I closed my eyes and thought of Mim while Jessica found her pleasure. We snuggled for a few minutes before I buttoned up my pants and raced back home.

The shower felt good against my skin, but no matter how much soap I used or how hard I scrubbed, I felt dirty. Jessica was right, once you removed any one of the reasons I gave myself for doing what I was doing, in the end, it was cheating, and Mim deserved more.

I closed my eyes and pictured her doing what River and Jade had done, and a fiery rage surged through me. I didn't want anyone touching her. She belonged to me, and only me. I'd never felt like a hypocrite until that moment. I was living the biggest lie of my life. How was I supposed to get through the next several weeks and be able to look Mim in the eye?

Dressed in jeans and a long-sleeved Henley, I sat in silence, thinking about my situation. I opened my wallet and pulled out the MBA coin. Professor Thieland's words ran through my head. *Keep your eye on the prize.* The problem was, I no longer knew what the prize was. Was it what I had originally thought important—debt free—employed—respectable? Or was the prize Mim? In my heart, I knew the answer, but my head wasn't in sync.

Close to eleven, Mim opened the door with the key I'd given her that afternoon. My parents looked exhausted, but Mom bubbled with excitement at seeing the show. Dad gave a curt 'goodnight' and walked toward my room, where he and Mom would sleep. Just the thought of what happened in that bed last night between me and Mim made me twitch with need.

My mother said her farewells and hugged Mim like she never wanted to let her go. "We're still on for tomorrow night?" Mom asked while walking down the short hallway.

"Yes, I'll pick you both up at six. We'll have dinner out and then see the Empire State Building and Rockefeller Square." Mim watched Mom close the door, and then she collapsed on the couch.

"Thanks so much for babysitting my parents." I pressed her back against the arm of the sofa and stretched her legs over my lap. I had another foot massage in me to give.

She leaned back and closed her eyes. "Your parents are great. We had so much fun, and believe it or not, I caught your dad smiling once tonight." She opened her eyes and watched me rub her feet. "You know the part where the animals parade down the aisle? Apparently, your dad likes giraffes."

"Who would have known?" I pulled her toward me, forcing her to scoot across the couch to my lap. "I missed you." I rained gentle kisses across her cheek until I reached her lips. With mine pressed to hers, I poured my love into her. Kisses were always the ultimate in intimacy for me. With a kiss, you could convey a message you couldn't describe with mere words. Locked in a kiss, you shared the breath of life.

"I missed you, too, but it wasn't a chore. Your parents are lovely. Besides, your mom has been telling me the dirt on you." She ran her hands up my sides and tried to tickle me. "Scared of monsters under your bed? Your mom says she gave you a can of Lysol and told you it was monster repellent."

"That's true. I still keep a can on hand just in case." She slid down my body when I stood up. "I should get you home." I helped her back into her shoes and walked her downstairs. After flagging down a cab, I put her inside, pressed two twenties into the driver's hand and watched her be whisked away.

____

Chapter 15

____

Mom never stopped talking about Mim. I got the impression she would have been fine not seeing me if Mim were around. Sadly, Mim had some work to catch up on, and my parents were stuck with me.

I skipped class, and we took a tour of my college campus, ate lunch at Katz's Deli and came home so Mom could rest up for her night.

Mim arrived, looking ready to conquer the world. Dressed in faded jeans, a red cotton tee, and a Yankees jacket, she looked like a local going to a game.

Mom ran to her and wrapped her in a hug. "This one's a keeper, Luca."

"I know she is, Mom, but I'm keeping her, not you." I pulled two hundred dollars from my wallet. It wasn't money I could afford to spend, but I couldn't let Mim cover the costs of entertaining my parents. In the scheme of things, a few hundred dollars was a rounding error.

"We're headed to the Empire State Building and then to Rockefeller Center to watch the skaters before the rink closes next week. I'm going to introduce them to the subway system." Mischievousness sparkled in her eyes. She lifted on her toes and kissed me. "I'll have my phone, so call me if you get a break." She corralled my parents out the front door. "Love you," she said before she closed the door.

Once alone, I showered and readied myself for the night. Dressed in my standard uniform of a suit and tie, I waited outside of Saju Bistro. Diane had chosen the place and was supposed to meet me at seven, but it was seven-thirty, and she was late.

"Sorry, I'm late." She arrived out of breath. "I tried to get a taxi, but it's almost impossible on Saturday night, so I attempted to take the subway, but two lines are down, so I had to wait until I could flag a taxi down. I need a drink."

"Let's get you a drink." With my hand on the small of her back, I escorted her into the restaurant. We were seated right away, and Diane wasted no time ordering a bottle of wine. "You look good, Diane." She was dressed in a form-fitting red dress and black heels. She could never be beautiful, but she looked like a woman and had a nice figure. "How's work going? Are you continuing to show the world the new you?" She'd worn her new heels the first week. The second week, she traded her trousers for a skirt. Week three, she let go of her boxy starched shirts and wore tailored blouses. By week four, she was dressing like a businesswoman, with full makeup and hair.

She emptied the first glass of wine, and the waiter immediately refilled it. I sipped on sparkling water. Unless this was an overnight job, which it wasn't, I never drank. People got sloppy when alcohol was involved, and I'd learned my lessons early.

"People are less shocked now. I got my first piercing and added earrings this week." She touched the lobes of her newly pierced ears. Tiny diamond studs sparkled in the low light of the restaurant. "I was asked out on my first date." She sucked down the second glass and refilled it herself.

"Did you say yes?"

She sipped at her wine and nodded.

I flagged down the waiter, and we ordered our meals. Food was an immediate need if she was going to walk out of here. Her nerves were obviously on edge because she didn't usually drink much.

I reached across the table and held her hand. "Are you nervous about the date?"

"Terrified. It's next Friday, and I don't know how to behave."

"Of course you do. You've been the perfect date for me. Just be yourself." I let go of her hand, which allowed her to pick up her drink and toss it back. "You should slow down. I'd hate for you to get sick." The truth was, I wasn't good with throw up. If she got sick, so would I.

She leaned into the center of the table like Jade and River

did when they wanted to censor our conversation. "What if he wants to have sex?"

"Are you afraid to have sex?" Was that why she hadn't asked?

"I've had sex, but usually I've paid for it, and you guys are required to tell a paying client how good they are in bed."

Laughter oozed from me because she was right.

"Let me tell you something about most men. Any sex is great sex. They aren't picky. Just let loose and enjoy the experience. Lay back and focus on the feelings."

"I feel sick." She launched from her seat and headed to the bathroom.

By the time she returned, dinner had arrived, but so had another bottle of wine. I was trying to send it back when Diane insisted on having another glass.

"You just got sick. You can't seriously want more wine."

Diane patted her pink cheeks. "I didn't get sick, I just got hot and needed some cold water. Maybe you're making me hot, Luca." She didn't lean into the center. Instead, she blurted out her sentence for everyone to hear. "This is our sixth date, and you haven't tried to screw me yet."

The waiter rushed over and asked us to quiet our conversation. Diane poured another glass of wine and told the waiter, "I pay him a lot of money to have sex with me, and he hasn't."

Amid the gasps and groans, I pulled out my credit card and paid for dinner. It was time to take Diane home. I'd bill her later.

"Let's go." I pulled her from the table and rushed to the exit. Once outside, I walked her away from the restaurant. If she was going to make a scene, better she make it in Times Square, where the crowd could drown her out.

We turned the corner onto Forty-second Street, where she pulled away and turned on me. "I pay you to do what I want. You don't get to decide. You have to do what I want. What I pay for." She threw herself at me and grabbed at my belt buckle.

"Stop it, Diane." I pushed her hands away. "You're drunk." The crowd around us was building. There's nothing like watching a train wreck, and Diane was drunk enough to look like one.

"Stop it? You started this. You changed me. You made me feel attractive, you made me care for you, and want you, and you've never tried to have sex with me. Why?" Tears ran down her face.

"Damn it, Diane, you're making a scene. If you wanted to get laid, all you had to do was ask. Remember, it's what you pay me for." Anger raced through my veins. Gripping her wrist, I whipped us around to escape the inquisitive stares of the crowd.

I. Froze. The air thinned, and the world spun around me. Standing in front of me was Mim, my father, and my mother.

A thousand thoughts rushed through my mind. *Oh shit, the subway line to Rockefeller Square was down.*

One look, and I knew Mim had witnessed every ugly word. How could I talk my way out of this? I rushed toward her. I'd never known her to be speechless, but she stood there, ripping my heart out with her silence.

"It's not what you think."

Diane stumbled on her heels and fell flat on her ass. "It's exactly what you think," she sobbed, red-faced and blotchy. "He's a male whore, but he doesn't put out for everyone. You're pretty, maybe he'll do you."

"Shut up!" I screamed. "Someone get her a cab." I looked up and saw my mother. Never in my life had I ever seen a look of disappointment cross her face. I was her pride and joy. I turned to Mim. "Mim, talk to me," I pleaded.

Mim looked from Diane to me. "Really, Luca? You have sex with women for money, but you won't make love to your girlfriend? Maybe I was using the wrong approach. Maybe I should have given you my checkbook instead."

"Luca, why would you cheat on your girlfriend? She is so good for you." My mother knotted the leather handle on her bag until it pulled free from her purse.

A quick glance at my father showed it was status quo. His head tilted a bit, but his expression was blank.

When my attention went back to Mim, she was mopping the tears that flowed uncontrollably from her eyes.

"Mim. Listen to me. It's not what you think." I was no longer able to justify what I was doing, not when I looked into the love of my life's eyes and watched the light in them dim.

"Stay away from me, Luca." She put her arms around my mother. "Let's go. I'll get you home."

I fell on my knees, reaching for her rapidly retreating body. "Mim, I love you, I really love you," I called after her, but she ignored me, shuffled my parents into a cab and sped away.

Chapter 16

I stumbled out of Times Square and walked aimlessly. A kaleidoscope of colors spilled onto the sidewalk in front of St. Mary the Virgin Church. What was waiting for me at home could wait a few minutes longer. I didn't know how I'd explain what I'd become and why. What I did wasn't who I was, or was that the lie I told myself?

I hesitated at the entrance of the church. Pulling the handle, I expected it to resist, but the door opened smoothly, as if it was waiting for me to enter. Silence filled the air around me. Not a soul was present, not even Father Tobin.

I walked between two pews and entered the lady chapel. Awash in the soft glow of light, Mary held her perfect son. The beauty of the scene moved me to contemplation. I pulled several dollars from my pocket and heard the clank of my coin hit the floor. I bent down to pick it up. Running it between my fingers, it felt heavy and cold. The coin that had driven my life forward now seemed like a weight on my soul.

I swiped at the tear that ran down my cheek and turned toward the life-size statue of the Pieta. My voice cracked, "Holy Mother, help me. I've made terrible choices in my life." I fell to my knees and sobbed. The understanding in her eyes gutted me. Prostrate in front of her, I spilled my sins.

With my cheek on the cold tile floor, I stared at the coin I hadn't been able to release. The letters were worn off from my constant caressing. MBA was no longer visible. In a moment of clarity, I realized it was no longer important. The quest for my advanced degree had blinded me to my reality.

I crawled to the candles and lit three more. Light flared from the Blessed Virgin like a benediction. After a final glance at the heavy silver coin, I slipped it into the offering box and walked away, feeling lighter than I had in years.

NOISE FLOATED under the door of my apartment. My prayers of having my parents in bed when I got home went unanswered. Mom was curled up next to Dad, her eyes swollen from the tears she'd shed over me.

She jumped from her seat when I entered. "What were you thinking, Luca?" Grabbing me by the collar, she pulled me toward the sofa and pushed me to sit on the coffee table. "Who was that woman, and what did she mean when she said you were a puttano?" My mother's shame was so great, she couldn't say 'male whore' in English.

I sat in front of them and hung my head in humiliation. I had to tell the truth. Hadn't there been enough lies?

"I'm exactly what she said. I have sex for money. She was an angry client who didn't get what she wanted."

Mom began to weep again.

Dad kissed her forehead and nudged her off the couch. "Stella, go to bed and let me handle my son."

My eyes flew to Dad's. "Handle me?" Fury raced through my brain. "For nearly six years you've ignored me, and now you want to handle me? Really, Dad?" I rose from the table so fast, it toppled over with a loud bang.

He glanced toward my closing bedroom door. "Luca, let's go to the pub down the street." He didn't wait for an answer, and I didn't argue. "We have a lot to discuss."

I ripped my jacket from the hook by the front door and stomped out of my apartment. How was it at twenty-six, he could still make me feel like a kid?

We walked in silence to Andy's Bar and Grill two blocks down. Luckily, there was an out of the way table still open. I didn't want to air my dirty business in front of a crowd. When the waitress arrived, I ordered a shot of whiskey and a beer; Dad stuck with beer.

He looked at me, rubbed the graying whiskers that had sprouted since the morning and sighed. "Why?"

I rubbed at my eyes and hoped the waitress would get here with my drinks right away. I didn't want to start this conversation without the support of Jack Daniels. Relief swept through me when she walked toward our table with a full tray.

I tossed back the shot and relished the burn that slid down my throat. "You ask why? I'll give you a why." I took a long draw of my beer and began. "I needed help, and I had nowhere else to turn."

"Why didn't you call?" Just call was the answer to everything, but it solved nothing.

"Call? You wanted me to call. Why? So I could tell you that you were right? That I'd graduated and had no income potential?"

"Being right doesn't make me any less your father, Luca. I would have helped."

I slammed my fist on the table. His beer sloshed over the side. "It's been nearly six years since you've taken any interest in me. Six years since I'd disappointed you enough for you to turn your back on me." He looked old and weathered. For a man of fifty, he hadn't aged well.

Unflappable as always, he sipped his beer and sat back. "Luca, I need to get something clear with you, and I want you to listen to me carefully.

"I built Gregorio Electric for you and your brothers. It was an early inheritance I expected you to accept with pride. When you didn't, I was understandably disappointed, but watching you make it through four years of college and ask for nothing? You proved yourself a man."

I dipped my head in shame. "I was drowning in debt when I graduated. Your words played over and over in my head. I graduated with over one hundred thousand dollars of debt, and the first job I was offered paid less than you did." I raised my head and pulled back my shoulders. If I were going to admit defeat, I'd do it with whatever remaining pride I could muster. "You were right all along."

"I may have been right about your initial income potential, Luca, but I was wrong about a lot of things. You took the hard route." Thinking about his words, he chuckled. "What I mean is, you acted like a man. You wanted something different, and you went after it. What father could be disappointed in a son who's motivated to seek better things for himself?"

Was he telling me he respected my choices? "You've acted like you were fed up with me the last six years. Why?" I lifted my glass as the waitress passed. I'd need another drink to get through this night.

"Was I acting disappointed, or was I giving you space you seemed to need? I don't recall you ever asking advice, instigating conversation, or seeking me out for anything. Your visits became infrequent, and avoidance was a skill you mastered."

I sat back and soaked in my father's words. In hindsight, he made a strong case. I was angry with him for not seeing my point of view, and I never considered his. I must have made him feel like his gift wasn't good enough, and he made me feel like my choices were wrong.

"I'm sorry, Dad. I wish we would have talked about it."

"We did, Luca, but neither of us was ready to listen. Tell me, son, how much money do you owe?"

I knew exactly how much I owed, down to the penny. I'd graphed it and logged it a thousand times. "I owe thirty thousand, four hundred and twenty-six dollars, and thirty-three cents."

His eyes lifted. "That doesn't seem like much. Why did you turn to this lifestyle when you owed so little?"

The waitress delivered two beers and a shot of JD. "When I left Chicago, I owed over a hundred grand. I knew I needed to put myself in the center of the financial world and get an advanced degree if I was going to have a chance in hell at making it."

"That's why you moved to New York?" He sipped his beer. "I'm a bit confused. You owed over a hundred grand, you obviously took out loans for this school. How much does an advanced degree cost?"

I wasn't sure I wanted to tell Dad how much money I'd spent. Would he change his mind and think I was back to being stupid and irresponsible? No more lies. "Between my undergraduate and graduate degree, I've spent over one hundred and ninety thousand dollars."

He choked on his beer. I waited to see if the light in his eyes darkened with shame, but it didn't. "You've paid off one hundred and sixty thousand dollars already? Tell me, son, how much money do you make?" His brows and beer lifted simultaneously.

"Three hundred and fifty dollars an hour."

He stole my shot and downed it. "You're shitting me?"

"Nope, that's the going rate for the service I work for. It's that or fourteen hundred a night."

"Let me clarify, you get three hundred and fifty dollars an hour to have sex with various women?"

"Yep." I nodded.

"Holy shit, son, I don't know whether to bow at your feet

or ask for your autograph. I'm in awe of you, but don't tell your mom."

It was funny watching Dad chime in on my shameful career choice. Instead of chastising me and making me feel little, he was proud.

Imagine that?

We shared a few more beers, and then stumbled back to my apartment. Dad embraced me, and I held on for longer than necessary, but it was nice to know we were back in sync. I felt less lonely, less vulnerable, and a lot more determined to make my dreams come true, and Mim Knight was at the top of my list.

"Thanks, Dad."

"I love you, Luca. I'll talk your mom off the ledge if she's still awake, but going to church tomorrow will make her feel better. Expect a lot of acts of contrition."

An audible groan escaped me. I wasn't ready for that. A willing confession was one thing, but willingly sitting down with Father Tobin and outlining each one of my sins would be painful and time-consuming.

Dad disappeared into my bedroom. After brushing my teeth, I sat down and texted Mim a short explanation.

Mim,

I should have told you from the beginning, but I didn't know how. Would you have dated me if you'd known? I doubt it. What I did is not who I am. I'm a man in love with one woman. I'm in love with you. I'm so sorry you had to learn about my ugliness this way. Please let me explain everything in person. It's too long a story to text.

I love you, Mim. Don't give up on me.

Luca

Several minutes later, she responded.

Luca,

I can't pretend what happened didn't. We have nothing left to say to one another.

Mim

She was wrong. I had a lot to say to her, and I'd find a way to make her listen.

Chapter 17

By six-thirty, I was sitting in the front pew of Saint Mary the Virgin Church, pinned between my mother and father like an unruly child. I fell on the padded kneeler and buried my face in my hands. Hiding was better than looking at Dad's awestruck expression, or the mask of my mother's obvious disappointment.

"Father?" Mom called to the priest walking by. "Father," she said a bit louder to gain his attention.

"Yes?" Father Tobin approached, and when he saw me, he smiled. "Hello, Luca. Nice to see you here."

Mom smiled with pride. The priest knowing my name would gain me favor. "When do you offer confession?" Mom was always direct and to the point.

"Mom. Stop." I pressed myself back into the pew. I couldn't hunch far enough down to disappear. "I'll go when I'm ready."

"Introduce us, Luca." Mom slapped me with a visual *where-are-your–manners.* Any favor gained by knowing the priest was lost.

I introduced Mom and Dad and prayed Father Tobin would rush off to get ready for the seven o'clock Mass we were attending. No luck.

"Luca says he's a regular at your parish, but getting him to confession has always been difficult."

Father Tobin eyed me when Mom said I was a regular. I was definitely going straight to hell. I'd be lucky if I didn't burst into flames on the spot. "Luca and I have had discussions about that very thing. He's promised to come in when he's ready." Father Tobin looked directly at me. "Open confession starts every Saturday at five, but for those who need more time, I'd recommend an appointment." There was no misunderstanding his words. Father Tobin knew I'd need a lifetime to come clean. "I have to go. It's a pleasure to meet you."

Relief covered me like a warm blanket. If I could just get through Mass, I'd be golden.

Up and down, I kneeled and stood like I'd done a thousand times in my youth. I kept my head low enough to avoid the stares of the Saints placed around the sanctuary, looking down at me in judgment.

When it came time for communion, I sat and watched parishioners pass me one by one, and I wondered if they assumed my soul was too tarnished to participate. My heart hammered when I recognized the man bowing in front of the priest. Marcus Knight received his communion wafer and waited for Mim and his wife. They turned to walk away but came to a dead stop in front of me.

"Mim," I whispered, barely able to breathe.

She lifted to her toes and talked quietly to her father, then walked straight out of the church. I rose to catch her, but Dad pulled me down.

"Son, give her space. Now is not the time."

———

MY MOTHER TALKED all through breakfast about Father Tobin.

"You will go to confession, Luca?" It was more of a demand than a question.

"Yes, I will."

She relaxed and ate. When she was finished, she reached over the table and took my hands. "Luca, you are a good boy, and nothing you did or will do in the future will ever stop me from loving you."

I'd thought every tear had left my body, but there was one remaining for my mother, and it slipped down my cheek in an endless stream.

"Thanks, Mom. I promise to make you proud."

"Luca, just make yourself happy, and I'll always be proud. And make things right with Mim. She's a keeper."

After breakfast, I placed my parents in a taxi headed to the airport. They offered to stay longer, but I needed space and a new plan.

MONDAY MORNING, I hid behind the large oak tree across the street from Mim's and waited for her to appear. The birds sang a ballad of encouragement from the tops of the trees. The sun shone rays of hope at her door.

When she exited the brownstone, I held my breath. Dressed in black slacks and a gray sweater, she looked beautiful. She locked the door and turned in my direction. Her hot tea was steaming on the top step.

She bent over and picked it up, then looked at the side where I'd written a message. I'd spent the night devising a plan. I needed to explain myself to her, and she wouldn't listen. If writing a note on her teacup every morning was the only way to communicate, so be it.

I snuck a peek around the gnarled bark. She was reading my note. I silently high-fived myself. The words I'd written echoed in my head.

Mim,

Nothing I say will take away the pain I've caused. The only place to begin is to say I'm sorry and try to explain myself. I've been a paid escort for two years. If I'm honest, I loved the job at first, what red-blooded male wouldn't? As time passed, I hated it. It diminished me as a man and a human. The plan was to earn enough money to pay off my student loans and be done. I never expected to meet you, but there you were, and you changed my life.

The words wrapped around the cup until I'd used every available space. Her blank expression gave nothing away, but she sipped my peace offering while she walked toward the subway station.

In my opinion, the morning had been a success. I'd felt on top of the world until I arrived at class and she was absent. That was the beginning of the rest of my shit day.

Sandra phoned after class.

"Luca, I just got a call from Diane. What the hell happened?" Her serpent tongue was loose, and I didn't need to deal with Sandra's venom right now.

"What did she say happened?" This might be worth listening to.

"She's accusing you of breach of contract. You need to fix this. I can't have my clients saying we didn't deliver what we promised." Her icy voice slithered across my skin. I was tired of being told what I had to do. My life was a screwed up mess, and all I needed to do was get Mim back.

"Breach of contract, really? That bitch drank herself under the table and then told everyone who listened, I wouldn't service her needs." *Unbelievable.* "She never asked for sex. She was all about the boyfriend experience. In fact, she owes me money. I had to remove her from the restaurant quickly and was forced to pay the bill."

"Luca, I've never said this to you, but you're a dick for hire. When you use your talents, there are never complaints."

"Damn it, Sandra. I turned Diane from a man to a passable woman. You told me she could be instrumental in determining my future, and you were right. She screwed up my life. While she was in a drunken puddle in the center of

Times Square screaming that I wouldn't nail her, my girl-friend and parents looked on."

"Luca, your personal issues are hardly my concern."

"They are now because I quit. I'll talk to each of my clients off the clock, except for Diane. The thought of seeing her makes me want to heave."

"Oh, Luca, stop being so dramatic. Finish with your clients as scheduled."

"No. I'm finished now."

There was no need to wait for her reply. I knew I was finished as an escort when I put down my coin. In all honesty, I was done a long time ago. My heart was never in it, but my mind had ruled my dick when it came to money.

Today, I'd begin a long week of letting go of my clients and burying my past. I'd meet with them once more off the clock to let them know I was no longer an option.

When I arrived at Laura's office, she was ready for me—the old me. I wanted to turn and walk away. The shame I felt for my actions was cinder block heavy on my heart.

"This isn't happening, Laura. I'm out." I picked up her jacket and tossed it over her naked lower half.

"What the hell are you talking about? Unzip your pants, and let's do this." She glanced at the window.

Bile rose in my throat, the acid threatening to choke me. "I quit." When I walked out, she was screaming a string of expletives that could make a sailor blush. "Bonnie, cancel all my mentoring sessions." Her mouth dropped as I left the office for the last time.

That wasn't how I expected our final meeting to go, but Laura wasn't a negotiator; she was a tyrant, used to getting what she wanted. I'd never made her anything but happy until today, and Laura unhappy wasn't pretty. Hopefully, the rest of the week would go better.

On Tuesday, I hid behind the tree and watched Mim pick up her tea. My chicken scratch covered the cup.

Mim,

My life began in Saunders' class. It ended in Times Square. I take full responsibility for my actions and for your unhappiness. Can we have dinner Thursday? We have to talk. I know a great Italian place near your house. Please say yes.

She sipped her tea and sat on the step. She pulled her phone from her purse, and the next thing I knew, mine was buzzing in my pocket. I fumbled for it.

No.

I'd never liked that word, but seeing it in bold letters was like a death sentence. Could a heart bleed out from sorrow? I was hemorrhaging each time she shut me out.

With my hands in my pockets and my shoulders creating a shadow I could follow, I trudged down the street away from her. Each step was like ripping a scab from a wound.

Twofer Tuesday would be a thing of the past after today. Meredith answered her door dressed in jeans and a cotton tee. The flowers in my hand were meant as a farewell gift, but she took them and gushed with happiness.

"It's been so long since I've received flowers." She brought the bouquet to her nose and inhaled.

"Men should buy more flowers." They were such a simple act of appreciation but were often overlooked.

Meredith set the flowers down and crushed herself into my chest. She reached up and tried to kiss me. "Meredith, I brought the flowers as a goodbye."

She stumbled back like I'd slapped her. This meeting would be hard because she had just made a breakthrough sexually.

"You're saying goodbye? Was I that awful?" She turned into a blubbering mess in seconds. Lines of mascara connected her eyes to her mouth.

"Meredith, this has nothing to do with you." I thought back to my do-as-I-say-not-as-I-do-words. "I told you to be honest about yourself with whoever you dated, but I didn't follow my own advice, and I ruined the best relationship I've ever had. My girlfriend found out about my job, and she left me. I can't continue to do what I did and hope to get her back."

"Are you lying to me?" She looked small and frail. "It's me isn't it?"

"You have no reason to believe me, but if I were a man making love to a woman, you would have been in the top one percent of women I'd made love to. Passion oozes from your every pore. You've got what it takes to make a man fall to his knees." I held Meredith for several minutes. When I left, I kissed her cheek. "Find someone worthy, Meredith."

Shelby was fine with our parting. She had a graph

hanging on her wall, and I was her mode of checking off every model car she could have sex in. She'd crossed out over a hundred and fifty so far. We'd never been able to find a Model T Ford or the Bat Mobile, but she was well on her way to reaching her goal. I'd brought her a model of a Shelby 350 GT, and we hugged goodbye.

For each client I let go, the heaviness weighing me down began to disintegrate. Once I let go of Jessica, I'd be free of my past. The question was, what would my future look like?

Wednesday morning, I left Mim tea on the doorstep and leaned against the tree in full view. She closed the door and stopped. Her eyes went to the tea, to me, and back to the tea. For a second I thought she would say something, but she picked up the steaming cup and walked away without giving me a second glance.

Mim,

As I write this, I'm thinking about Hester Prynne. She sinned for love. I sinned for money. Despite my shortsightedness, my eyes are fully open, and my love for you will never die. I've said goodbye to my past. I'll leave you with this quote from The Scarlet Letter. "She had not known the weight until she felt the freedom." I'm free, Mim.

I arrived at Judith's house with a bag of groceries. Chicken piccata was on the menu. I had the breasts she planned to tell her friends I'd felt.

"Luca, you make an old woman happy." We walked through the entry and straight into the kitchen. Once I had her seated at the island, I went to work.

"I hope you're hungry." I opened the silverware drawer

and gasped. The forks and spoons had been switched back. "Someone else has had their hands in your drawers."

She dismissed my comment with a wave of her hand. "I could only be so lucky. What is this about you dropping me as a client?"

I walked around her kitchen like a blind man reading Braille. I touched everything until I'd found what I needed to cook her dinner.

I inhaled lungfuls of regret and exhaled mouthfuls of resolve. "Oh, Judith, I totally messed up." Once I explained the situation, she *pffted* and waved me off again.

"Luca, you are not canceling our Wednesdays. We have a lot to accomplish and so little time." She sipped on the glass of white wine I'd poured her.

"What kind of things do we have to accomplish?" Confusion filled my eyes. There had been no mention of a plan, but obviously, Judith had one.

Her voice rose in exasperation. "Luca, you're a young man who needs a job. How do you think it's going to work out when you show up at the offices of the women you've been sleeping with? Will you be able to look at them as your boss, or will you imagine something else?" She shook her head and rolled her eyes. "In theory, the dean's list is an excellent concept, but in reality, its only function is to provide short-term income."

I'd always figured I wouldn't run into any of them. My entry level position wouldn't have given me access to the women I'd been sleeping with for months. I never thought that far ahead; all I knew was I needed a job.

"I haven't given it much thought, but unemployment is not an option."

"Luca, remember when I told you that you were so much more than even you knew? The very best attribute for a person to have is likability. People like you and you like people. It's obvious in everything you do. You showed up here knowing you'd quit. Why come in person when you could have called?"

"I felt I owed it to you to explain in person why I would be abandoning you in the future." I never considered anything but a face-to-face meeting.

"That takes courage. How many of these meetings have gone badly?"

"One. She wasn't used to hearing no." I chuckled at the memory of hearing Laura scream her frustration.

"I want you to meet someone at my company. I believe you'd be a valuable asset to Kent International." Judith pulled her cell phone from her pocket and began to type. "I'm going to set up an appointment for you. Even if you're not interested in working for Kent International, the interviewing experience will be good for you. A good interview is a foot in the door."

"Really, Judith, you don't have to do that for me. Besides, what could I possibly do for Kent?"

"All those millions of precious stones turn into cash, Luca. I imagine you are excellent at tracking cash flow. Am I right?" She looked down at the large diamond that graced her left ring finger.

I'd been a professional bean counter for years without

realizing it. "Yes, I am magnificent at following my cash flow. I know where every dime I've made has been spent."

"You would be good at many things. Opportunity knocks on many doors. It's knocking on yours."

I dredged the chicken and chopped the shallots while Judith and I discussed my future. By the time I'd finish cooking our dinner, she had scheduled me a tour and an interview at Kent International.

We ate in the beautiful dining room decorated in soft yellows and robin's egg blue. The wallpaper pictured open cages and birds fluttering about. If I had let my imagination go, I could have pretended I was in an aviary and the birds flew free around me.

After we had eaten, I cleaned up and asked Judith if she'd like to meet the following week. This wouldn't be paid time. It would be me spending time with a woman I respected, someone who expected nothing but my presence.

"Luca, you're not getting rid of me that easy. Let's have dinner in the city next Wednesday. You can tell me all about your day at Kent Enterprises. Invite Mim if you'd like."

After a kiss on Judith's cheek, I climbed into a taxi and headed back to the city, full of chicken and warmth.

Chapter 18

There were no classes, no clients, nothing on Thursday. I'd left Mim chai tea and a single red rose on her doorstep. I leaned against the rough bark of the old oak tree and waited for her to appear.

The door opened, and Mim emerged, but she wasn't alone. Her dad stood beside her. She bent over to pick up the flower and tea when our eyes met. She took a step toward me. Her free hand lifted in an almost wave, and her lips turned into an almost smile.

I pushed off the tree and stepped toward her, She wavered, and her half-smile faltered. She turned and walked away with her father. My heart sank with every step she put between us. Today's note was simple.

Mim,

I've never been in love until I met you. I'm not sure if it was immediate, or it happened over the course of our relationship, but the night I told you I loved you was the most honest thing I'd ever said. I love you, Mim, and I refuse to let you go. I'll spend the rest of my life proving I'm a good man if that's what it takes.

Love, Luca

With my hands buried in my pockets, I entered the subway and went home. Mom would be calling soon. She phoned daily to make sure I was okay. The biggest surprise was, Dad had been calling, too. He wasn't a big talker, so it didn't take long to catch up on the six years we'd missed. Despite the crash and burn of my life, some positive things had come out of the experience. I'd mended fences with my father, and with every day that passed, I was mending fences with myself.

The smell assaulted me immediately. My apartment was trashed again. On my way to the kitchen table, I stepped over a knee-high pile of clothes that needed washing. My living room had become my laundry basket. I knew I had to pull myself together. What I wore today was the last clean outfit I owned.

There wasn't a clean dish or glass in the cupboard. I'd begun to cup my hands and drink water from the sink.

I needed to get myself together. I would get Mim back, and when I did, I wanted to bring her into a clean home. I wanted to make love to her on clean sheets, and I wanted the next day's breakfast cooked in a spotless kitchen.

My fingertips were pruned by the time I'd finished cleaning, but the results were worth the effort. I pulled out a frozen helping of spaghetti and meatballs Mom had made, and I sat at my clean table to eat it.

When I powered up my computer, the spreadsheet flickered to life. Falling short by thirty thousand dollars wasn't too bad when I put things into perspective. I had twenty-two thousand dollars in savings, the money I'd need to hold me over until I could find a job. I'd never done the math before, but I'd had sex over four hundred times to pay off the bulk of my college debt. At roughly a teaspoon of ejaculate per event, I filled over eight cups in my tenure as an escort. I laughed at the thought. Jessica would have been ecstatic.

It was the silly things that made the day go by fast. Who else would measure the amount of come they'd expelled in two years?

Enough procrastinating.

Pulling off my nails with pliers would have been infinitely easier than writing my graduate project report. Every word reminded me of Mim. The rise in stock prices made me remember the rise in her anger at seeing Diane. Dividends reminded me of the less than stellar results I got from my decisions. Bonded, merger, and long-term were things I wanted with Mim.

Against my better judgment, I sent her a text.

Mim,

Thinking of you and missing you. I met with Judith Kent, and she invited us to dinner next Wednesday. Can you make it?

I love you.

Luca

I thrummed my fingers across the table and waited. By the time she responded, my pads were numb.

No, Luca. I can't do it. Please don't tell me you're doing Judith Kent.

I was such an idiot. Of course, she would think I was doing Judith.

Mim,

Judith is just a nice woman who likes my company. We eat and talk. That's it. She liked you and wanted to get to know you better.

Can you cut me some slack? I'm trying here.

Luca

Would Mim ever let the past go? Five, ten, twenty years down the road, would I be paying for a decision I made when I was twenty-four?

I'm trying too. I'm attempting to fall out of love with a man who broke my heart, and each time I see you, the wound begins to bleed. It's killing me, Luca. No dinner for me, but tell Judith hello. My father says if you're bringing tea he'd like a double shot latte. By the way, what did you do to him? He now seems to be standing in your corner.

Seeing me was causing her pain. A pain I could relieve with my absence. It would kill me, but I'd give her more space. And as for her father, I was baffled.

I'm sorry Mim, I never meant to hurt you. I only wanted to love you. I'll bring you coffee and tea and give you space.

Love always,

Luca

When I arrived at Mim's, her worn copy of *The Scarlet Letter* sat on the steps. I picked it up and hugged it tightly to my chest. It was the closest thing to Mim I'd touched in a while. I left the tea and coffee on the step and walked away with renewed hope. Today's cup held a simple message.

I love you.

Love, Luca

On her father's cup, I wrote a short note.

Thank you for your support.

I could only assume Marcus Knight saw something in me he respected.

By seven, I was sitting in Jessica's house, drinking beer and watching her while she packed. She'd need a suitcase for her sex toys alone. Out of all my clients, she was the best. She'd become a friend and mentor, and her fetish had paid off a huge amount of my debt. I'd always remember her with fondness. Leaving her was easy. It was time, and we both felt the pull of our futures tugging us forward.

The next several days, I stayed away from Mim and spent my time working on my report and looking for employment. Landing job interviews was a priority, and I'd had two, but nothing seemed promising until I met with James Seagull from Kent International. The corporate office was located in the heart of the financial district, a block from the

New York Stock Exchange. The lobby was black marble, with wall niches that held millions of dollars in precious gems.

Kent International's main source of revenue was mining, but they dabbled in many industries from healthcare to manufacturing.

"Luca, it's great to meet you." James shook my hand with the confidence of a king.

"Happy to be here. Although, I'm not sure why I'm really here. Judith just told me to show up, and I did."

"It always goes better for those who do what Judith says." His voice held humor that I appreciated. Too often, men in positions of influence lost their ability to laugh. I hoped that no matter what I lost over time, my sense of humor wasn't included.

"She's a determined woman." I was meeting her for dinner in the city tonight, and I imagined we would talk about the company she was so proud to own.

"That she is. Let's take a tour, and I'll tell you why you're here."

We walked along the wall, where James explained the gems, where they were mined, and what their significance was. I've never seen a diamond come in anything other than black and white, but the cases held blue, green, yellow, orange, brown, purple and red. The colors were based on the impurity that entered when the stones formed.

"When something outside the norm is mixed in, beautiful things can happen. That's where you come in, Luca." We entered the elevator and were rushed to the twenty-fifth floor. "Judith has decided in her golden years to give back to the community that gave her so much."

"She's a generous woman." Judith had asked nothing of me except for my friendship. We'd had a lot of fun coming up with naughty things to tell her friends, like my hands in her drawers and on her breasts. She was smart, charming, and witty.

"In this day and age, there are few opportunities for college students to earn and learn. She's worried about the next generation, and that's where you come in. Judith wants you to oversee the Kent Center for Opportunity."

"The what?" Generally speaking, I was good at following people, but James had lost me at the word 'oversee'.

"She wants to open a center that helps college students find suitable employment during school and after graduation."

I shook my head. "I'm a finance major. I know nothing about finding jobs. If I did, I wouldn't be unemployed."

"It's not much different from stock trading. You'll be given a certain amount of money, and how successfully you invest that money will determine how many people you can help. You'll hire who you need and provide a service students can use." He closed the door to his office. "Luca, I made my way through college as a stripper. I would have done anything to get out of school debt-free, and I did, but it would have been nice to have had other options."

Did he know my story? If so, he didn't judge me. He understood me. "I know about the lack of opportunities."

"Luca, you now have options. I believe you're meeting

with Judith for dinner. She asked me to give you this offer and told me she would be happy to discuss the details tonight." He handed me a fancy Kent International envelope. "Obviously, Judith sees something special in you, or she wouldn't have chosen you as her project."

"I'm assuming you were once her project?" The envelope felt like hope wrapped in fine linen paper.

"Yes, and now I'm the president of her New York Office. I may be premature in saying this, but welcome aboard, Luca. If Judith wants you, you have to have something special."

"She says I have heart."

He gave me a half-smile. "Well, nothing stays alive without one."

Fifteen minutes later, I sat in a coffee shop down the street and stared at the envelope. I'd always assumed I'd make six figures, but I couldn't begin to put a value on what Judith wanted. This envelope contained my worth in Judith's eyes.

I tore through the paper and opened the trifolded page.

Dear Luca,

I'm an old woman, but I'm a smart woman. I know quality when I see it. I saw it in my husband so many years ago when I convinced him to marry a poor country girl and let her make him a millionaire. I see it in you.

The secret to success is seeing value in people. It's not in the fancy suits they wear or the jewelry they drape themselves in. Value is seen in an honest heart, and a desire to please.

Your annual salary will be one dollar. I am offering you a one hundred thousand dollar sign on bonus, and each year you will be paid a bonus based on your success.

I'm not giving you a job, I'm offering you an opportunity. Good things come to those who fight for them. Are you a fighter?

Sincerely,

Judith Kent

CEO Kent International.

I reread the letter twice. She'd offered me the most valuable dollar I could ever earn. I'd thought graduating debt-free would earn me respect, when all it took was being myself.

My parents were responsible for my windfall. They had taught me the importance of a kind word, a smile, or a helping hand. "It's not what you have, it's what you give," they always said.

It took me about six seconds to sign the acceptance part of her letter, and about an hour to get Mom off the phone after I called and told her I was employed.

My first paycheck was going to my parents, and they would frame and cherish that dollar forever.

I walked into the steakhouse on Madison Avenue and scanned the room for Judith. She sat smack dab in the center. The candlelight danced off the large ruby brooch pinned over her heart. I was overwhelmed with emotions, gratitude, and hope.

"Luca," she motioned for me to sit beside her. "Let's celebrate." She ordered champagne, and we toasted to my future. She pulled a crisp dollar bill from her pocket and slid it across the table. I defaced it by signing my name across the front. I'd put it in the mail to my parents tomorrow.

We enjoyed a relaxing dinner while we discussed her expectations. My first day on the job would begin the day after graduation. Until then, I'd work on finishing my degree and working on a way to get Mim back into my life.

Chapter 19

Mim's text came in late on Sunday night.

Luca,

Are you okay? I haven't seen you in a long time. I miss my tea.

Mim

I rolled over in my bed and cradled the phone to my heart. It was the first time she'd reached out to me in weeks, and I wasn't sure what to do.

Mim,

I've been busy. I'm due to give my graduate report tomorrow. After that, I'll tie up some loose ends, and I'm finished with school. Sorry about the tea, you made it clear you didn't want to see me, and I was respecting your wishes.

I love you,

Luca

Nothing else came in even though I stayed up watching my blank screen.

In the morning, I packed up my graphs and loaded my presentations on a thumb drive. I had two prepared. One if Mim was present, the other if my audience was a bunch of dodgy old professors. One would get me a passing grade in the class, and the other would clear my conscience once and for all.

I slipped my hand in my pocket and stroked the red felt E. It wasn't the cold coin that once weighted me down. It was soft and warm and would be an important component of option two.

Judith had asked if I was a fighter, and in all honesty, I didn't know, but I was ready to go all twelve rounds if it got me one moment to prove myself to Mim.

At two o'clock, I took my place on the stage. The spotlights made it impossible to see who was in the audience. I squinted and strained to see the faces of the bodies in the first row, but it was impossible.

Inhaling deeply, I smelled lilacs. Mim was here.

Her voice floated through the air. "Mr. Gregorio, do you have the required number of reports available?"

My knees nearly buckled from the sound of her voice. She was here, and that meant option two would be implemented.

Five folders containing my project were handed to the beautiful woman who approached the stage. Before she could pull away, I said, "This is for you. I may not graduate, but I don't care. Nothing will ever mean more to me than you."

She pulled the folders from my hand, "Good luck, Luca," and she disappeared into the darkness.

Who would have thought I'd put it all on the line for a woman? Six years, I'd chased a dream that included debt-free, employed, and respectable. How does a man become an escort and remain respectable?

The flash drive slid seamlessly into the computer, and with the touch of a key, my first slide appeared.

Are You Getting What You Paid For? Commodities in the Twenty-First Century.

"Ladies and gentlemen, today you're going to hear something you won't hear every day. I'm going to talk about commodities of a different type. I was told I had thirty minutes and I could discuss anything I wanted. So without further delay …"

The paper backing peeled off the felt E, and I pressed it to my chest. I'd considered an A, but I'd never serviced married women, so E for escort seemed more appropriate.

"I'm Hester Prynne with a penis." A gasp came from the black hole in front of me. "Two years ago, I stepped out of the norm to sell a commodity that's been sold for thousands of years. I sold myself."

I brought up the graph I'd been keeping for twenty-three months. "As you can see, I obliterated over one hundred and sixty thousand dollars of debt by using particular talents."

"Excuse me, Mr. Gregorio." I recognized the voice of

Professor Saunders. "Are you going to tell us that you worked as a…what do I call it?"

"Whore, gigolo, prostitute, escort? You can call it anything you want, in the end, it's all the same. I sold my body for money." Mumbling filled the auditorium.

"I have to say, you've intrigued the board. Continue."

No doubt, I interested the board. People are closet perverts. What they won't come out and admit to in public, they devour in private. I had first-hand knowledge of the many fetishes people enjoyed.

"As you can see from the graph, I've had a lot of sex. At three hundred and fifty dollars an hour, I'd have to have had a lot of sex to earn the kind of money I did."

Mim piped in. "Did you say three-fifty an hour?"

"Yes, or fourteen hundred a night." I wished I could see her face. "Is there any way to turn down the spotlight? It's blinding me." Moments later, the light was lowered and I had a clear view of my audience—four male professors and Mim. "Thank you."

One of the professors I didn't recognize asked a question. "How did you find a job like that?" Was he asking out of disbelief or curiosity?

"I was recruited on this campus. I'm not going to discuss the company or people, but I'll talk about the job. If anyone approaches me about this conversation, I'll deny it ever happened. This would probably go better if we used a question and answer forum."

Mim stood and walked to the stage. "How could you take

advantage of those women? You used their bodies for money." She crossed her arms and held her position.

I rubbed the E on my chest. "You have it wrong. I didn't call them. They called me. They used their money for my body."

One of the professors began to speak, but Mim stomped her foot and glared, silencing the man. "How could you have sex with strange women but never sleep with the girl you claimed to love?" The men behind her mumbled.

My voice wavered, then steadied. This was Mim's greatest hurt. She'd felt I'd given to so many others what I wouldn't give to her, and she was right, but she was wrong, too.

"Sex was mechanical for me. It was a job. Not unlike the job you do grading papers for Saunders."

"We are not talking about papers, we're talking about a couple connecting and being honest with one another." The murmuring continued, but Mim put a stop to it with an evil glare and loud shush.

"Yes, we are. In complete honesty, I refused to dirty the woman I loved for selfish need. I wanted her so badly, but I wanted her the right way. In my mind, having sex with her at the same time as having sex with a client was the ultimate in disrespect. Every day I went to work, I was a day closer to making love to her. She was my reward."

Mim's arms dropped from her chest to hang loosely at her sides. "You lied to protect yourself."

"Yes, I lied to protect what we had. I lied by omission, but look at what the truth did to us."

"Was there anything that was special for us?"

"When I kissed you, I poured every bit of passion and love into you that I could. I've never kissed a client. My kisses were saved for you."

"What about sexual safety?" It was clear she was referring to the time I tasted her. I closed my eyes and remembered the moment when her body soared, and I held her while she cascaded down from her climax.

"Barriers are used for everything from sex to oral sex. No skin-on-skin action." I wasn't going to tell her that I came all over Jessica's chest because I'd never actually touched her; only my fluids did.

Relief washed over her.

"Really?"

"There are rules, and I followed them. Testing is free, and I did that on a regular basis. Although the risk of me contracting something was almost nil." Every fiber in my body wanted to jump from the stage and pull her into my arms, but I respected her personal space.

"Your clientele, were they only women?"

"Many escorts see both men and women, but I only saw single professional women."

"Why the E?" Mim was quick with her questions.

I rubbed the E I'd stuck over my heart. "The woman I love likes *The Scarlet Letter.* During one conversation, she told me society judged too harshly. I'm hoping this will be a visual reminder to judge me fairly." I pulled the top and middle lines from the E, leaving an L. "When this is over, I may graduate, or I may not, but I'll walk out of this room knowing I left nothing unsaid, and I'll carry all the love in my heart for you, Mim. I love you. I always will."

I collected my belongings and walked toward the stairs.

"Mr. Gregorio?" Professor Saunders stood.

"Yes, sir?" I turned and focused on the man who resembled a rock legend more than a teacher.

"You've stunned us, but I think there's a story here. I imagine you could write a book. *The Scarlet Letter* is already taken, but you're a resourceful man, and I'm sure you could come up with something." He chuckled. "In all seriousness, what's next for you?"

A smile danced on my lips. "I secured a job. My annual salary is a dollar, but the bonus potential is incredible. Right now," I looked at my watch, "there's a priest who's reserved several hours of his time for me. Life is looking up." I glanced past Saunders to Mim. "I hope I'll see you soon, Mim. You know where to find me."

I was finished. Each trash can along the way received a piece of my past. My gym card, my medical insurance card, my flash drive, and the pieces I'd torn from my E were all thrown away. I was leaving the past behind and walking into my future.

I reached up to peel the L off my chest and changed my mind. I'd wear my scarlet letter with pride. There was no shame in wearing your love outside your heart.

Father Tobin had prepared for my visit. He had a full pot of coffee ready and some cookies on a tray. Lord, was I going to be here long enough to miss a meal?

"Father Tobin, I've never been to a face-to-face confession. I'm at a loss." I'd always walked into the confessional and blurted out my sins in relative privacy.

"It's no big deal, Luca. We're just two friends talking. Have a seat." I paced the room that was devoid of scowling saints. The only presence was Father Tobin, a statue of Mary, and me.

Three hours later, I was exhausted but wired. I'd drunk three cups of full octane coffee and ate every cookie from the plate.

I had several acts of contrition to complete before I was as clean as a new penny, but I'd made it through the worst of it. I didn't go to confession to empty my soul; it was more of a cleansing of my conscience—a coming to terms with who I was, and who I wanted to be.

My body rocked in front of Father Tobin. I wasn't sure if I should shake his hand, keep my distance, or embrace him. The man groaned when I wrapped him in a bear hug and squeezed.

I SAT at the front of the church. The beads slid through my hands as I recited my third Hail Mary. When I bent to retrieve them from the tile floor, the scent of lilacs swirled around me. I closed my eyes and prayed.

A hand reached down and took mine. My heart raced. Hope bloomed inside of me. Slowly, I opened my eyes, and bliss warmed me from within. My prayers were answered.

"Mim, what are you doing here?"

"I thought I'd kneel beside you and lend my support. How many do you have left?" She twined her fingers with mine.

"One more, and then I'm finished. I think the three hours I spent in his office granted me grace."

"I'm proud of you, Luca. What you did today took courage. I have a thing for courageous Italian men." She pulled the rosary through our fingers. "Let's do this last one together."

I didn't know why Mim was here, but the fact that she was, was a miracle, and I was in a place where miracles could happen. We ran through the beads with efficiency. After the last "Amen", I tried to swim in the softness of her eyes. I wasn't sure where this moment would leave us, but I hoped it wouldn't end.

"What now?"

Her eyes sparkled with mischief. "I know it's far below your average, but I have a hundred dollars." Her cheeks turned pink.

"You are not sitting in church, offering me money for—"

"Of course not. I'm offering to take you to dinner." She toyed with my hair, making tingles skitter down my spine.

"I'm starving. Where are we going?" The red L glowed under the bright lights of the church.

Mim reached for it, but I stopped her from pulling it free. "No, I like it. I don't know if you'll ever want more with me, but I'll wear this every day to prove my commitment to you. There is no shame in loving you."

"Luca, I'm sorry. I didn't handle that well." Her shoulders

rounded like an aged woman. "It's not every day a girl finds out her boyfriend is an escort."

"Your reaction was understandable." I pinched her chin and raised her face to meet mine. "I should have said something, but there was no benefit in divulging my dirty secret. I feared I would lose you, and it happened anyway."

"Oh, Luca, if the man upstairs can forgive you, who am I to argue?" She leaned in, and my heart hammered in my chest. When she pressed her lips to mine, the world stood still. My hands ran the length of her back and gripped her hair, pulling her closer to me.

"Mim." I groaned. "I love you."

Her mouth opened, and I wasted no time brushing my tongue against hers. I made love to her mouth with more passion than ever before. Breathless and shaking, I broke away.

"Let's get out of here. I'm starved, Luca, but not for food. Are you ready to give me more?" She pulled me by the arm toward the big wooden doors.

"I'm willing to give you everything."

Could she hear the booming of my heart? Each beat was a declaration of my commitment to her.

Chapter 20

Cabs were easy to flag down when you were desperate, and I was desperate to be alone with Mim. I tossed a twenty at the driver when he pulled up in front of my apartment.

We ran the three flights of stairs to my door. I fumbled with the keys until she ripped them from my hand and jammed them into the lock. Mim had no problem with being direct.

I ran my hands down her arms and basked in the beauty of her presence. "Mim, tell me what you want." I couldn't risk any misinterpretations. If she left me again, I would be crushed beyond repair.

Gripping both hands, she pulled me to the bedroom. "I want you. I want all of you." She stopped inside the door of my room. "Isn't it time I got you all to myself?" Her expression wasn't accusatory. It was loving and warm.

"I don't deserve you but I want you."

"I know." She nipped at my lip. "I'll make you deserve me, Luca. You're a good man who was lost. My father has reminded me of that every day since we broke up."

"I'm glad you found me." We walked toward the bed, and I pulled her shirt over her head. Pink lace covered her perfect breasts. I ran a finger over the lacy edge, and her breath hitched. "I'm going to do to you what I've never done to anyone in my life."

She pulled at my jacket, tugging it off my body. "What's that?" She tired of plucking my buttons free one at a time and yanked my shirt open. Little white disks flew through the air.

I shed my shirt and gripped her hands. "I'm going to make love to you." I picked her up and placed her in the center of my bed. "God, you are exquisite." Today wouldn't be rushed. I'd put her off for so long, dreaming of this day— this moment. It would be criminal to race through it.

I toed off my shoes, pulled off my socks, and climbed on the bed next to her. She pulled my finger into her mouth as soon as I touched her plump, kissable lips. Energy surged through my veins. All I could imagine were her lips wrapped around my hard shaft.

Picking up her hand, I sucked each finger until she squirmed beside me. "Luca, I need you."

"Baby, you have me."

"Now."

"Nope."

"We're doing this again?" She stilled and bolted upright.

She must have thought I was going to hold her off once more. "Nope." My erection strained against my pants until I dropped them and set it free. "We're doing this for the first time." I slid onto the bed next to her. "You only get one first time." I brushed my lips across her neck and up to her ear, where I whispered, "I want it to be special."

Her body shivered under my touch. Her skin prickled when I grazed my fingers under the edge of her bra. Her nipples rose to peaks beneath the lace. I pulled one cup down and replaced it with my mouth. When I latched onto her nipple, her hips rose from the bed.

My free hand pushed her down and skimmed the outside of her panties. Stroking her through the lace, I could feel the dampness of her arousal. The slow pace was killing me, but her shallow breaths drove me forward.

One-handed, I pulled her underwear free and dipped my fingers into her sweetness. I remembered her taste, and I craved more. Her sounds, her scent, her feel, called to me—screamed at me to dive in and take what was mine, but my heart told me to slow down. Mim deserved an experience that would wash any doubt that I loved her away.

I slid from the bed and took one of her feet. The last time I'd kissed them, her toenails were painted pink. Today, they were red. Passion red, like the flush that covered her skin. When I pulled a toe between my lips, she pulled away and giggled.

"No, no sucking my toes." She reached down and pulled at me to move up her body. "Are you into that?"

I pulled her foot to my mouth. "I'm into you, Mim, and I

want to get intimately acquainted with your entire body." Her foot flexed when I ran my tongue up her instep. After several minutes of massaging, I moved on to her ankles. They were small and feminine. I kissed both of them and moved to her calves. Long walks across campus and hours at the gym had given her shapely legs.

The backs of her knees were sensitive. I loved the way she squirmed when I ran my mouth across the crease of her knee. When it came to her thighs, they were works of art. No sculptor could have done a finer job than nature did. All I could think about was those thighs squeezing my hips. My dick twitched, pressing me to move forward in my exploration.

Her hipbones, her belly button, each of her ribs steered a path to her heart.

"Mim, I want to bury myself in your body, but more important to me is burying myself in your heart." A quick tug, and her bra fell free. My lips found their home on her left breast, as physically close to her heart as I could get.

She moaned as I pulled the puckered bud into my mouth and caressed her other breast with my free hand.

"You broke my heart, and you mended it." She pulled me up by my arms and pressed her forehead to mine. Her sharp blue eyes pricked at my soul. "My heart is yours, keep it safe. I love you, Luca. I have since that day I told you to ride out the storm, and you said it was a damn tsunami." She licked at my lower lip. "You're a damn hurricane, Luca, but I love you anyway. Now make love to me."

I grabbed a condom from the nightstand and rolled it

over my aching length. Poised above her, I nudged at her entrance. Never taking my eyes from hers, I watched her melt into the sheets as I pressed deep inside her body.

I'd had sex hundreds, maybe thousands of times, and nothing ever felt like Mim did. She completed me in ways I couldn't have imagined. She challenged me, she frustrated me, and she loved me. She was right, I didn't deserve her, but I had her, and I was never letting her go.

***

ONE WEEK LATER, Mim and I were lounging on her bed. I was writing my business plan for the Kent Center for Opportunity while Mim graded the last of Professor Saunders' papers.

"Oh my God," she yelled. She bounced up and down, causing her laptop to plummet to the carpeted floor.

I bolted upright, sending my notebook flying across the bed. "What? What's wrong?" Something significant had occurred.

She leaned over the bed to pick up the computer. The blanket fell from her luscious bare hips. The world could be ending, and I no longer cared. Mim was naked in bed with me, and all was right in my world.

She opened her computer and pulled up the final grades for Professor Saunders' class. "Look." She pointed to my grade, barely a C. "You passed." She dropped the computer and climbed into my lap. "My hot Italian stud is going to graduate. I'm so proud of you."

"Mim, there was a time where making money, earning respect, and graduating were the focus of my life." I rested my hands on her hips and pinned her with a look of love and devotion. "Those things are great, but they're not important. You opened my eyes, and you opened my heart."

"Are you seducing me, Mr. Gregorio?"

"No, I'm loving you the best way I know how, with my mind, my heart, and my soul."

"Add your body, and we have a long-term deal." She sank onto my hardened length and made love to me.

For good or bad, The Dean's List brought me to this point—to this woman—to this magnificent moment. I might have barely graduated, but I'd graduate with honor—my honor, and I'd have Mim by my side. She was a keeper, and she was mine.

____

A Sneak Peek at The Learning Curve
TWENTY YEARS AGO
____

Coco Chanel had it right when she said, "There are people who have money, and people who are rich." The people she forgot to mention were those who were neither—the poor bastards living paycheck to paycheck, borrowing from Peter to pay Paul. I was one of Coco Chanel's forgotten, but I planned to change that.

The Paul in my life was tuition, rent, and groceries. I'd maxed out my loans. I'd maxed out my credit cards. I'd maxed out my options. I was down to living off hopes and dreams. Three-quarters done with college and fully committed to finishing.

I glanced at my watch—a Timex. I endeavored to be like its slogan: _Takes a licking and keeps on ticking._ Like this watch I'd dropped, washed, and lost a dozen times, I was no quitter.

My last-ditch effort was this meeting with the dean of the school. I'd hounded him with fifteen letters, twenty-two phone calls, and a five-hour sit-in in the reception area of his office. The letters went unanswered, and the calls were not returned, but the sit-in did the trick. He took one look at me and scheduled an appointment. It turned out that his secretary was taking the summer off to tour Europe and he was looking for a temp.

I gathered my things and raced across campus to his office. What I lacked in experience, I made up for in determination.

I had no idea what the job entailed, but I was game for anything. A summer job would keep me from returning to the commune. I was finished with community gardening and free love. I wanted more. I wanted the power and control that came with a degree.

The glass ceiling was there; it sparkled and shone and gave you a glimpse of a possible future, but it was bullet-proofed. There was no way to break through if you were a woman with limited means. All I knew was that Dean Hollings held the power when it came to this school, and power was something I craved. Hopefully, he'd offer me the job.

In front of his door, I pulled it together. I pinched my cheeks, straightened my skirt, and applied fresh lip gloss. After a long, cleansing breath, I walked inside. Something told me today was the start of something big.

I announced myself to the prune-faced secretary: "Sandra Tierney to see Dean Hollings." She dropped the pen from her thin, gnarled fingers. Fingers she no doubt worked to the bone day in and day out. She'd typed the fat pads right off them, leaving bony tips that looked like unsharpened pencil nubs.

The nameplate on her desk said, *Greta.* An old-fashioned name. The woman stood, her back so hunched over, I was certain she'd been born at the turn of the century. Her soft-soled shoes squished across the floor until she came to a squeaky stop in front of Dean Hollings's door. She tapped twice and opened it.

"Ms. Tierney is here to see you," she said with a slight tremor in her voice.

Was it fear or old age that made her words tremble? Dean Hollings didn't strike me as a man to fear. He was a man to revere. He ran an elite university that educated some of the greatest minds in the world.

"Send her in."

The deep tenor of his voice pushed a ripple of something up my spine. Maybe he could instill fear. I wanted to believe I could be the one to intimidate—that I could take charge of any situation—that I would be more than a secretary or a waitress. I wanted to be a woman who ruled her world, but as much as it bothered me, I needed the help of a man to get me there.

"Close the door, please," he said without raising his head. He shuffled through a few pages on his desk, then looked up at me. "Come here."

My heels clicked out a staccato rhythm across the tile. With my head held high, I marched to his desk. I didn't balk at his demand. I did what I was told. The dean didn't come across as a man I should question.

Younger than most men in his position, he didn't get there by not hunting down what he wanted. If he wanted me at his desk, I'd be there. I looked at his dark hair and stared into his whiskey-colored gaze. He was easy on the eyes, successful and sexy all rolled into one.

He rose to his feet and pointed to the leather sofa against the wall. I walked to the sofa and smoothed my black pencil skirt over my thighs. I adjusted the side slit so only a peek of my bare skin showed when I took a seat. At first, I tucked my legs to the side, which was the most ladylike way to sit. But then I crossed one leg over the other because it made me feel more feminine, and I noticed how his eyes lingered from the slit of my skirt to my calves.

His height and width loomed over me like a dark cloud, hardly the way I wanted to start this interview. "Are you going to stand?" I asked.

He narrowed his eyes and looked between the couch and me like he was at war with himself. The leather cushion won.

Air rushed up as the cushion compressed under his weight, catching the smell of his cologne and spreading it like an atomizer through the air.

This man wasn't Old Spice or dime-store cologne. He was old money. It showed from his argyle socks to his silk tie.

"What can you do for me, Ms. Tierney?"

I loved the way he said my name—the hard *T* followed by a whisper of the rest.

My heart skipped a beat, and my nerve faltered. I had no

idea what I could offer him. All I knew was that I'd gotten in the door after thirty-eight attempts.

Takes a licking and keeps on ticking.

"I'm in trouble, Dean Hollings." I'd never been a weak woman, but I thought I'd play the damsel-in-distress card first. "I'm one year away from graduating with my business degree, and I fear I can't afford to finish." I tried to summon a tear, but I wasn't a skilled thespian, so I rubbed at the corner of my dry eye for effect, hoping to play on his sympathies.

He kept looking at my legs and licking his lips. "You need this job."

My sigh lifted and sank my shoulders. Damsel in distress and sympathy weren't working. It was time to stroke his ego. "You're the most powerful man on campus." I lowered my head and let my hair curtain my face. "I thought maybe…"

He slid forward and pushed the strands behind my ear. "You thought what, Ms. Tierney?"

I licked at my red apple lip gloss. His eyes followed the tip of my tongue. "I thought I'd be a good fit for your summer position. I need a job, and you need an intern."

He sat back and raised both brows so high, they disappeared under the fringe of his dark brown bangs.

"Intern?" He shifted on the cushion until he faced me. "I was thinking more of a temporary hire. Bringing you in as an intern implies I'd be your mentor." His knee brushed against my thigh. "What experience can you bring to the position?" He pulled his lower lip between his teeth and rolled it back and forth.

"I'm responsible, motivated, and a quick learner."

"Do you have experience?" The way he asked made me think he was asking about more than my typing and short-hand skills.

"I can take notes and type and answer phones. What I don't know, I'll learn. I aim to please." The last time I'd needed something fiercely, I'd slept with a man for a used car and a semester of paid tuition. "I really need this job. I'm desperate." The words had a breathy Marilyn Monroe wispiness to them I didn't recognize, but I sure welcomed it.

"Desperate can be dangerous." His eyes went to the closed door. "Where's your family?"

"I'm an only child, and my mom lives up north." To be more accurate, she lived at a nudist colony. She couldn't help me. She had less than I did. She would have loved for me to stay with her, but I had bigger dreams than organic gardening and free love.

"I was an only child, too." He pulled at his tie and leaned back, gaining distance from me, but his eyes never left my face.

"I grew up with a lot of other kids around."

Living in a place where everyone slept with everyone produced a lot of children. Mom was protective and kept the men away from me until I turned seventeen, the age of consent. After that, I was allowed to choose for myself. Little did she know, I'd been having sex since I was sixteen with Daniel Ockey, a boy I walked to school with each day. You couldn't live in a nudist colony with hundreds of wagging dicks around and not be curious. We fed our curiosity every day after school behind the barn.

"So what you're telling me is, you know how to play nice in the sandbox."

"I can play nice when I have to." I uncrossed my legs and watched him watch me. "I'll do what I have to in order to get what I want."

"What is it you want?"

"I want it all, Dean Hollings. Every inch of everything life can offer me." I leaned back and looked at him.

His amber eyes had turned to dark chocolate. A bead of sweat formed on his brow. "Can I call you Sandra?"

"Of course." He could call me anything as long as he hired me.

"I have another interview today following this one. The person I select has to be open-minded and available."

I placed my hand on his leg. "Please choose me," I whispered. My fingers skated across his slacks until my hand dropped from his knee.

He cleared his throat and looked at his watch. "Sandra, I —" He glanced at the door and then at me.

My time was finished, clearly. "I'm sorry I've taken up so much of your time, Dean Hollings." I gathered my purse and walked to his desk. "I'll leave my phone number just in case you have more questions. I'm positive I could be an asset to you over the summer." I scribbled my number on a piece of his stationery. "I'm good at typing and oral ..." I let it hang there for a minute while I finished writing the last two digits of my phone number, "... dictation," I finished.

I walked to the door, turned around, and smiled. "See you soon." I closed the door behind me.

Someone once said that when a man was attracted to a woman, she became his weakness. I had never fully considered the power of being a woman—until recently. A man with the right appetite could provide a girl with what she wanted. All she needed was the drive to pursue what she desired and the balls to take it.

I didn't wake up and think, *I'll seduce the dean for a job.* It seemed to happen without thought, although in hindsight he did seem taken with me during my sit in.

When he swept my hair back, I realized it wasn't the touch of a concerned administrator. It was the touch of a would-be lover.

Mom always told me the key to influencing men was to keep them coming back for more. She bartered for things like orgasms. The stakes were higher for me: I *needed* a job, but a quiver in my girly bits would be a nice bonus. Or maybe I could negotiate for a scholarship. That was a thought. A pleasant one. Lord knew I'd given more for less.

Well, I'd planted the seed, and now it was time to leave. It would work or not. Either way, I was no worse off than when I came in. I'd leave here a girl up to her neck in debt with one year of college to complete—exactly as I entered. Or maybe I'd get a call that said, "Let's barter."

"How did it go?" Greta asked with a hopeful expression.

I let out a little giggle and looked over my shoulder at the dean who was adjusting his trousers. "It's hard … to say."

Get a free book.

Go to www.authorkellycollins.com

About the Author

International bestselling author of more than thirty novels, Kelly Collins writes with the intention of keeping love alive. Always a romantic, she blends real-life events with her vivid imagination to create characters and stories that lovers of contemporary romance, new adult, and romantic suspense will return to again and again.

For More Information
www.authorkellycollins.com
kelly@authorkellycollins.com

Acknowledgments

I was humbled by the number of people who fell in love with The Dean's List. I had intended for the book to be a stand-alone, but after countless emails asking for more, I knew that Luca's story had to be told.

As always, I am grateful for the fans that read, review, and spread the word. It takes a village to raise an author.

Jodi Henley, this book would have been less without your editing skills. Thank you!

Love and hugs to my family who are always there to lend an ear or offer advice.

9 781955 379946